Joey's Angel

JANE BONANDER

JOEY'S ANGEL
Copyright © 2025 by Jane Bonander

ISBN: 979-8-88653-421-4

Published by Satin Romance
An Imprint of Melange Books, LLC
White Bear Lake, MN 55110
www.satinromance.com

Published in the United States of America.

Cover Design by Ashley Redbird Designs

To my late Aunt Ethel, who began her teaching career at Old Glory, a one room country schoolhouse in Highlanding Township, Minnesota

Prologue

Early September 1866
Northern Minnesota

J oey Prescott licked his palm and pressed it against the stubborn cowlick that sprouted from his crown. He looked at his father's dark, wavy hair. "Wish my hair was like yours, Pa." They rode side by side in the wagon toward the community building, which was currently being used as the church and temporary schoolhouse.

Sam Prescott studied his 10-year-old son. He favored his mother, no doubt about that. The straight black hair, the high, proud cheekbones and the regal nose. Pure Dakota— or Sioux, as the whites called them, a name they didn't like for it meant "enemy."

Only Joey's eyes gave him away. They were blue. "Blue as the waters of the north," his mother, Laughing Eyes, used to say with affection.

1

Laughing eyes. Something hard and angry always pressed against Sam's heart when he thought about his wife. He felt responsible for her death, even though he could have done nothing to stop it.

He had been away fighting for the union when a few restless, hungry young Dakota Braves, out for revenge against the whites, sparked a bloody revolt that left many dead on both sides, including his wife.

Newspapers had called it the Great Sioux Uprising, slanting its views against the Indian, not allowing anyone to know the real reason behind the war. But Sam knew there had been hunger, anger and a feeling of betrayal among his wife's people. Even so, most of them had not wanted the confrontation.

When Sam had returned from the war between the states, the wife he reluctantly left behind, his sweet Laughing Eyes, was dead, killed by his own brother during the uprising. May have been an accident; Sam would never know for sure. But that hadn't prevented him from nearly beating his brother to death. His family had naturally taken his brother's side. They had never approved of his marriage to a "filthy squaw" and hadn't taken to Joey as grandparents should. The rift between Sam and his family had widened, and Sam had taken Joey and moved north. There had been nothing left for him but harsh memories in the southern Minnesota lands that had absorbed the blood of so many.

The trouble was, no matter where they went, prejudice against the Indian followed.

"I'm happy with the way you are, Joey," Sam said. "Each time I look at you I'm reminded of your ma."

Joey glanced at him. "Does it hurt when you think about her, Pa?"

Sam smoothed his hand over Joe's cowlick. "Not like it used to, son." All he wanted on this earth was for Joey to be happy. That he was half Indian shouldn't matter. He was an innocent boy who didn't understand the slights and mockings of others. Speak of the devil, Clarence Nisbeth's boy Ernest was kicking around a ball with another boy near the school building. He bullied Joey any time he saw him unless Sam was with him. Once Joey came home with a black eye.

Joey saw him but ignored him. "There's the building, Pa."

Sam noted his son's quiet enthusiasm, almost felt the intense excitement that coursed through Joey's body. He hadn't dared approach the school board about allowing Joey to attend. He knew he had a better chance if Joey just showed up. He'd thought this was the first day of the new school year, but as he looked around, he began to wonder. Other than Ernest and his friend, there was no sign of other children. Everything was too quiet.

"So it is. Nervous?"

Joey nodded, his eyes riveted on the white clapboard building. "Some."

Sam reined in the team. "Have a good day, Joey. See you this afternoon."

Joey gazed at his father, his light eyes showing a hint of fear. "By, Pa."

Giving him a reassuring smile, Sam handed him his lunch pail. "You'll do fine." He watched his son walk stiffly to the building, climb the stairs and disappear inside. Maybe he should have accompanied him the first day.

Ernest swaggered up to Sam, that cruel smile on his lips. "Ain't no school for him."

Sam ignored the kid. Instead, he studied the building wishing he were a fly on the wall. Joey was tough. He could handle himself. But a part of him ached for his son, because he knew that all his life Joey would have to fight harder for his share of what the world had to offer. Then the door opened, and Joey stepped outside.

Sam and his son locked gazes briefly before Joey looked away. Sam saw the rejection stamped all over his son's handsome face.

Slowly Joey descended the stairs and trudged toward the wagon. When he reached it, he stared again at his father, tears filling his eyes. "They didn't want me, Pa."

Cora Nisbeth looked up from her knitting and studied the three men standing at the window, one of them her husband. They were foolishly staring after the half-breed child they'd just refused entrance to the school. She quietly clucked her tongue but forced herself to say nothing.

Her husband, Clarence, turned and shook his head. "It ain't right. If God wanted man to breed with the Indians, he'd have civilized them." Cora glanced up at Henry and Oscar Hassler, two other members of the school board, and knew that they, like Clarence would never change their minds about the Indians. Every farmer for miles around had run-ins with them at one time or another. Prejudice ran deep.

"The boy was quiet and mannerly," she said softly, "his father probably isn't a bad sort."

Clarence pressed a pinch of snuff between his cheek and gum. "How would you know, woman? They live out there, every bit as antisocial as Torkelson and that breed squaw of his. They come into town and don't speak to a soul. Not a living soul."

"Well, we haven't exactly made him feel welcome." She glanced around her, remembering that just the day before, they'd all gathered in the building for the church service. It made her feel guilty at her unchristian like behavior toward the man and his half-breed son. Whether Sam Prescott had married an Indian woman or not shouldn't make a whit of difference. He was a human being, just the same, and God probably still loved him. The least they could do was act civilly toward him.

She'd thought of Eve, the young girl they had brought home from the orphanage four years ago, who was now the new teacher. Her teacher's training had given her newfangled, outspoken, often outrageous ideas she'd hoped to implement in the classroom. "I have a feeling if Eve were here, you'd have a fight on your hands."

"Lucky for her she wasn't," Clarence said, turning a harsh eye on his wife. "And we don't need your two cents worth, Cora. You are not a member of this board. Eve Engles will do what she's told, if she wants to keep her job."

Cora wasn't the least bit offended by her husband's blunt words. She merely sniffed at him and went back to her knitting.

The Hassler brothers, who owned land near the Nisbeths, exchanged glances but said nothing. Cora knew they agreed with her husband. They all had cause to be wary of the Indian. It was just that...well, she didn't feel that a child should be punished for the sins of his father.

Oscar Hassler held a newspaper he'd been reading earlier high in the air, as if it were some kind of divine torch. "I read it before, and I'll read it again." He brought the paper down to eye level, pushed his glasses to the end of his nose and began. *"The Indians, the Sioux and the Chippewas, are having a high old time again, killing each other at every opportunity. May that opportunity be every minute of every day. May they kill each other until the last savage is dead, and we're rid of their dirty hides forever."*

Cora's fingers flew over her knitting; She could always knit like a house of fire when she was angry or upset. "Have you forgotten that little half-breed's father owns the land you want to build a new schoolhouse on?"

Clarence frowned at her; she knew that look. It said, "Wife, when will you learn to keep your mouth shut?" She pursed her lips and glanced away.

We'll find other land, then," Clarence grumbled, turning again to the window.

She wanted to ask what harm it could possibly do to let the boy attend school. But she also understood her husband's reasons for not allowing it, and in some ways, she couldn't blame him. His only sister and her family had been killed by Indians. It would take a miracle to change his mind about any of them.

Chapter One

Early November 1866

S he should never have stayed at the school so late; she should have left with the others. There would be plenty of time to prepare the pageant. Christmas was still more than six weeks away. And storms like this were not unheard of this time of year.

Shivering, although she was dressed warmly, Eve Engels trudged through the deep drifts, the cold, sharp wind hammering snow at her face, instantly numbing her skin. Putting her hand to her mouth, she sucked in her breath, grateful her mitten filtered out some of the cold. She brought her scarf across to cover everything except her eyes, then continued through the morning snow, against the screaming, ice-filled wind, in the direction she thought would bring her to the Nisbeth home.

She slogged through the drifts, her heart pumping with

the exertion. Squinting into the wind, she saw nothing. The Nisbeth barn should be directly in front of her. A bubble of fear froze in her chest as she realized she'd somehow lost her way. She'd known it was possible. It was easy to get lost during a snowstorm. The wind could easily blow a person off course.

Her legs were numb to her knees, and she could hardly feel her toes. Shielding her eyes, she looked hard into the distance. A fluttering of hopes spiraled through her. Was that smoke? The outline of a cabin?

Praying it wasn't an illusion she forced her feet to move on. Relief lifted her heart when she saw the definite outline of a log building. It wasn't the Nisbeth place, but at least it was shelter. She was afraid she'd taken a wrong turn some-where; she couldn't see a thing.

A dog barked, the sound muffled by the swirling flakes. As she approached the cabin, the sound became louder, until suddenly the animal was upon her, yapping and whining at her heels.

"G-g-good doggie," she stuttered, shivering against the cold and her newly found fear. She reached out, allowing the animal to sniff her mitten. He playfully bit the end, pulling it free. She gasped as the icy air hit her hand, then gave a startled cry when the animal licked her fingers.

"Good dog," she said again as she picked up her mitten and moved toward the darkened building. "Is this your house?" Barking a response, the dog led the way to the cabin door.

She knocked, flinching as pain shot through her knuckles. No answer. With her mitten at hand, she pressed the latch and opened the door, finding it dark inside except for a fire burning in the fireplace.

Shuddering with anticipation, she scurried into the room, allowing the dog inside before closing the door against the invading wind.

She stood only a moment before crossing to the fireplace. After turning up the embers, she laid more wood over the top, then stood back and watched it catch. The dog snuffled noisily at her side before dropping down in front of the flames.

She removed her wet felt boots, her coat, her mitten and scarf and draped them over a chair by the fire, then sat down next to the dog. She looked at the animal and laughed quietly "Well, a fine watchdog you are."

He gazed at her through his long, hairy eyebrows while his furry tail thumped against the floor.

She removed her apron and wiped off the dog's wet back. "Oh, I don't care what you are or whose you are. You saved my life."

Exhausted from her journey through the blizzard, she pulled a blanket off the back of a chair, curled up in front of the fire and fell asleep.

"Sure is snowin', ain't it, Pa?" Joey's voice was muffled as it came from beneath the thick, warm quilt they were wrapped in.

"Worst storm of the year so far," Sam answered, feeling Joey huddle closer.

"Sure is a good thing the horses know the way home, ain't it, Pa?"

Sam could barely see the horses up ahead, pulling the small sleigh through the snow. "Smartest horses in the state, son."

Joey poked his head out from beneath the quilt. "We should be hearing Chancy by now, shouldn't we?"

Sam listened for the dog. Hiding his concern, he answered, "He's probably found himself a warm spot next to the chimney and is sound asleep."

"I hope he ain't froze to death," Joey murmured, igniting Sam's own silent fears.

"Chancy's too smart for that," he answered, hoping to reassure the boy.

The horses stopped in front of the barn. Knowing his duty, Joey followed his father out of the cocoon of warmth and helped unhitch the team.

"I don't hear him, Pa."

Sam heard the frightened caution in his son's voice. "Let's get the horses fed and bedded down, then we'll have a look, all right?"

Minutes later, Sam and Joey waded through the snow toward the cabin.

"Here Chancy!" Joey's voice was caught up by the wind and carried away. "Chancy! Here, boy!"

He tugged on his father's sleeve. "Where is he, Pa?"

Sam hated the thought that had eaten at him since they'd neared the farm and hadn't heard the dog. Chancy had already had run-ins with a wolf and a skunk. Unfortunately, he never seemed to learn his lesson. Though Joey attributed his pet to the wisdom of a sage, Sam knew Chancy was just a dog.

Sam pushed the latch on the cabin door and stepped

inside. His gaze was drawn to the fireplace. Startled and dumbfounded, he answered, "Chancey's here, Joey."

Man and boy inched toward the fireplace, stepping silently. A pretty, blonde haired woman lay there, wrapped in Joey's quilt. She was asleep, one arm beneath her head and the other resting on Chancy's back.

The dog raised his huge, hairy head and gave them a baleful look as his tail thumbed against the floor.

Sam stopped, unable to move.

Joey inched closer, finally pausing in front of her. He sighed and slowly shook his head. "I'll be dogged. She looks like an angel." He turned, giving his father a puzzled look. "Where do you suppose she came from, Pa?"

Sam shrugged out of his sheepskin jacket, hung it on a peg by the door and ran his fingers through his wet hair. His gaze moved back toward the hearth, and the beauty who slept there. She did have the face of an angel, and her hair... White gold strands had settled on her cheek, the light from the fire igniting them.

"She must have gotten lost in the storm." His gaze moved over the rest of her, and he couldn't help noticing her fine, womanly shape. Even through her clothing he could detect round, full hips and a generous bosom.

"Can we keep her, Pa?"

The longing Sam heard in his son's voice was like a knife to his gut. It pained him to know Joey needed more than he could give him.

"I'm afraid she probably belongs to someone else, Joey." Joey kept staring at her as he sat and removed his leather boots. He rubbed his toes through his wool socks, ignoring the holes. "She sure is somethin', ain't she, Pa?"

"She sure is," he answered on a heavy sigh.

The young woman made a little sound in her throat, sending Joey scrambling backward. Chancy lifted his head again and licked the woman's face. She frowned and blinked, moaning slightly as she sat up.

Her gaze moved slowly toward them, and she pressed her hands to her mouth and gasped. "Oh! Oh, my!" She stood quickly, her frantic gaze moving toward the door. "I'm... I'm sorry. I... it was snowing so hard. I lost my way..." her voice trailed off as she looked at Sam.

It's alright, ain't it, Pa?" Joey stood before her, grinning like a fool.

"Glad we could be of help." Sam studied her, wondering who she was. Though he and Joey kept to themselves, Sam couldn't believe he'd have missed seeing her. Not that it would have made any difference; white women usually avoided him like a storm of locusts when they discovered he had a half-breed son.

She cleared her throat, breaking into Sam's thoughts. "I guess I should be going..."

"You can't go out now," Joey argued. "It's still snowing something awful, ain't it, Pa?"

Sam crossed to the window and looked outside. "I am afraid so, ma'am. I won't take my horses out again. They've been through enough for one day."

She was silent behind him, and when he turned, he caught the fear and uncertainty in her eyes. His gaze moved lower, over her ample breasts, then down over her hips. When he looked at her again, she was watching him.

"I certainly can't stay here," she murmured, sounding both frightened and perplexed.

Sam wanted a drink but opted for coffee. "Joey, I'll bet the lady would appreciate a cup of coffee. And put Chancy back outside."

The woman gasped. "You're not going to make the poor animal sleep out in the blizzard, are you?"

Joey's eyes lit up. "Yeah, Pa. Can't Chancy sleep inside? Just for tonight?"

Judging by the look in the lady's eyes, Sam thought she wanted Chancy as a bodyguard. Ah, hell. What harm would it do? "All right. Just for tonight, then."

Joey's grin widened as he went to prepare coffee for their guest.

Rubbing her arms nervously, she went back to the fire, her back to Sam.

"Joey thinks you dropped out of the sky, just for him."

Turning, she gave him a puzzled look. "Excuse me?"

He nodded toward Joey. "My son." He grinned at her, enjoying her look of confusion. "He wants to keep you."

Her look of startlement was replaced by a shy, tentative smile. "Oh. Yes, I... I seem to have that effect on all boys under the age of ten."

He wanted to argue that he couldn't imagine men of any age not being affected by her. Wisely, he kept his mouth shut. He'd been rebuffed too many times by too many women even to consider saying it.

Suddenly a frown nicked her smooth, flawless brow. "Shouldn't your son be in school?"

To avoid her gaze, Sam glanced away. "He should be, but he isn't."

"But why?"

Sam barked a laugh. "You obviously didn't get a good look at him, ma'am."

"I can tell that he's of school age," she answered tartly. "I suggest you bring him to my classroom at your earliest opportunity."

Sam's insides froze. "Your classroom?"

She stepped back from his glare. "Yes. I'm... I'm Eve Engels, the school mistress.

Chapter Two

E ve watched the change come over the man's handsome face. Anger and some private hatred suddenly hardened his features.

"So, you're the school mistress. Well," he said around a snarl, "take a good look at my boy, ma'am, and then tell me you've never seen him before." Eve swallowed a blister of fear. The boy, Joey, came toward her holding a mug of coffee. He had a wide, innocent face, and she immediately saw his Indian features. Her gaze drifted slowly to the man standing beside him. So, she thought, pressing her hands against her heart, this was Sam Prescott, the man who had married an Indian woman. She'd heard about him. Somehow, she'd pictured him differently. Wilder, maybe. But she hadn't listened much to the gossip. Considering her own dubious background, having been left on the steps of a Minneapolis church as a baby by a girl who couldn't face the consequences of her act, Eve had always felt she was the last person to judge another.

She gave Joey a tentative smile and accepted the coffee.

She took a sip, hiding her grimace as she tasted the strong brew. When the boy retreated back into the depths of the cabin, she turned her gaze on the father. "I have never seen either of you before."

His eyes changed from expressing anger to revealing nothing. Turning away briefly, he answered. "Whatever you say, ma'am."

"You don't believe me."

"It doesn't matter what I believe. What's done is done."

"What do you mean?" For the first time she really took stock of his features. Amending her earlier assessment, she realized he wasn't truly handsome. His face was too hawk-like and his eyes too piercing. His hair, wet from the snow and messed from the wind, was dark, and far too long to be fashionable. He was tall and lean hipped, though wide through the shoulders and thickly muscled.

She didn't think he was an Indian, but it was as if he'd lived with them so long, he'd absorbed their peculiarities. It was pure conjecture. She had no idea if it were true.

"I took Joey to the school, and he was turned away."

Eve bit her bottom lip and felt a rush of sympathy. She understood rejection. "When was this?"

"The first part of September. I don't recall the exact date."

Eve realized he must have brought his son to the building during a board meeting. "School didn't start until the end of the month."

"Well, someone sure as hell turned him away."

"I'm sorry. I wasn't there that day. If I had been, I—"

His humorous laugh interrupted her. "It wouldn't have mattered."

Stung, she bristled. "How do you know that?"

He went to the hearth, nudging the dog aside with his toe before turning up the fire. "Where have you been living, anyway? In a convent?"

"These are good people, for the most part," she answered, understanding his sarcasm.

He lifted a wood chunk into the grate. "But they still hate Indians."

"Can you blame them? I mean, some of them had families down south, around New Ulm. They lost their loved ones in the massacre."

"The Indians lost loved ones, too."

"But the Whites didn't start all the trouble," she argued.

He turned and glared at her, his stance almost vicious. "Have you any idea why it happened in the first place?"

She moved toward the dog and stroked his furry ears. When she stopped, the animal nudged her hand with his nose, so she continued. "Only what... What others have told me and what I've read in the papers."

He jabbed at the fire, seeming to find an outlet for his anger. "I've often wished the Indians had a similar means of communication. But I guess even if they had, no White would ever read it."

"Why do you say that?"

"Because it's true. As you read the papers, did you ever get the impression that the massacre happened because the Indians were hungry? That they were waiting for long overdue money promised them by the government? That all the land the Whites reaped had once been theirs? That they'd been confined to a small reservation, pressured to abandon their culture and religion?"

Eve swallowed. It sounded too...reasonable. If that had been the case, wouldn't someone have mentioned it? "Still, there's no reason to kill innocent people."

He sighed and dragged his hand over his face. "You're right, of course. What no one understands is that reason had nothing to do with it."

"Did you live with the Indians?" she ventured.

"For ten years," he answered softly.

So, she'd been right. She crossed to the window, the dog following. It was still snowing and blowing. The wind howled mournfully. Suddenly she remembered that she couldn't leave. Turning swiftly, she caught him studying her.

"I really can't stay here," she whispered.

A hooded expression crossed his face. "You'll be perfectly safe. You can have my bed; I'll sleep in the loft with Joey."

Her stomach was in knots, and her mouth was dry. Turning to the window again she knew she had no choice but to accept what he offered.

She glanced at the bed in the corner where a patched quilt was spread carefully over the bedding. Her stomach continued to roil. It wasn't that she was afraid of this intense, angry man. Something inside her had been drawn to him immediately. She'd always found widowed men who were forced to raise their children alone very appealing. It was partly because it made them vulnerable—which she sensed most men wanted to hide. It also reminded her that her own parents, whomever they were, had refused to take on their responsibility.

"I don't see what there is to think about," he said, breaking into her reverie.

Taking a deep breath, she faced him, finding his whole bearing darkly intriguing. He'd unbuttoned his shirt and pulled it from his jeans, exposing the top of his long underwear. Hair, dark and curly, peeped out over the stitching, and his firm chest muscles were outlined beneath the fabric.

Oh, there is much to think about. She took another dizzying breath and looked away, willing herself to focus on chaste thoughts, like puppies and babies and innocence. But puppies and babies dredged up reminders of how they were conceived, and all thoughts of innocence fled.

Bringing a hand to her throat, she swallowed, scolding herself for her wayward thoughts. "You're right, of course." She glanced up at the loft; the boy was on his stomach, staring down at them, his eyes wide.

Suddenly her stomach growled, and she knew that Sam Prescott heard it. Her cheeks flamed.

He gave her a quick glance, then cleared his throat. "I'm...er...Joey and I ate supper with some friends. I'm sorry. Can... can I fix you something?"

With the nervous shake of her head, she answered. "No. Really, I'm not hungry. I am... I'm fine."

"Well, if you're sure." He gave her a gruff sigh, then nodded toward a dry sink near the bed in the far corner of the room. "You can clean up there, if you want. There's a clean towel on the rod."

Still clutching the fabric at her throat, she gave him a nervous nod. "Th- thank you. I'll be fine." She waited until he'd taken the ladder to the loft, then scurried to the bed and crawled under the covers—fully dressed except for her shoes.

She could hear father and son stirring above her, trying

to get comfortable. The boy's whispers were met with short answers in Sam's deep voice, and she knew the conversation was about her. She rolled to her side and took a deep breath, pulling the smell from the flannel bedding into her lungs. The private, masculine scent triggered a response from deep inside her, and she drew the bedding closer. This was his smell. Not unpleasant at all, it was strangely comforting and... provocative.

It had been years since she'd left the orphanage. Years since she'd had to share a bed with anyone. Lying in this man's bed, surrounded by his scent, was far more pleasant than sharing her bed with two other squirming girls or sleeping alone.

Eve had slept hard. When she awakened, it was still dark, but the fire had been fed, and she knew it was morning. She was also hungry. She crept from the bed and looked toward the loft. They were gone, probably out in the barn doing chores.

After quickly washing her face and hands, she hurried to the kitchen corner of the cabin and rummaged through drawers and bins, finding the fixings for breakfast. By the time Sam Prescott and his son returned from their chores, she'd sliced and fried salt pork and had batter cakes bubbling on the griddle.

"See, Pa? I told you she'd have breakfast ready."

They both stamped the snow from their boots, then left them by the door. Joey strode to the table, his eyes closed and his nose in the air, noisily pulling in the warm, delicious smells.

"Um, boy. It sure smells good, ma'am," Joey said.

Eve smiled, but it vanished when she looked at the boy's father. From beneath his dark brows his eyes glittered dangerously.

"Joey, wash your hands and face," he ordered, his gaze still on Eve. "You didn't have to make breakfast."

She quickly flipped the battered cakes. "It was the least I could do," she answered, aware that her pulse was racing. When she turned back, he was at the dry sink and Joey was at the table, face scrubbed and hair brushed to the side, although a stubborn cowlick rose from the top of his head.

He eyed the crispy salt pork and licked his lips. "Hurry up, Pa. I'm hungry."

Eve heaped the batter cakes onto a platter she'd found in the makeshift cupboard and set it down in front of Joey just as the boy's father came to the table. His sleeves were rolled up, exposing hard forearms covered with thick, dark hair. She stared, marveling at the corded muscle that strained at the taut skin.

Blinking furiously, she looked up and caught him watching her.

He immediately began rolling down his sleeves. "I'm sorry, ma'am."

Flustered, she cleared her throat. "Oh. No. Don't be. I mean, I don't care. I mean, you don't have to roll them down..." She stopped, aware that she was babbling. "Please," she finally said, "sit down and eat."

He sat, and to her surprise, he and Joey bowed their

heads and recited a prayer in a language Eve didn't understand.

Moments later, Joey was praising the breakfast to the heavens. "Umm- mmm. I ain't never tasted such good griddle cakes. Have you, Pa?"

The man swallowed a mouthful of food. "Since we're having a genuine school mistress to breakfast, son, I think you should think about proper speech."

Joey gave his father a puzzled look. "Huh?"

"Maybe it's time to stop saying 'ain't'."

Eve lowered her gaze to her plate and hid a smile.

Joey nodded. "Oh, yeah. 'ain't' ain't, I mean, isn't a very good word, is it, ma'am?"

She smiled. "No, it isn't."

They finished breakfast in silence. As father and son cleared the table, Eve said, "I fried up the ends of the salt pork, and there are a couple of batter cakes left. Is that... I mean, can they be fed to the dog?"

"Yeah," Joey answered. "Chancy'd love it, wouldn't he, Pa?"

"He'll think he's died and gone to dog heaven."

"Aw, Pa,' Joey said around a laugh. "He always gets table scraps. They just ain't—I mean aren't as good as these."

"Alright, son." His father returned the smile. "Take it out to him and feed him in the barn."

When Joey left the cabin, Eve found Sam Prescott at her side, helping her clean up the kitchen. He must have noticed her surprise, for he said, "We've been doing this ourselves for years, ma'am. I'd feel funny letting you do it alone."

Eve couldn't believe her ears. This man was, well, she had to face it, *perfect,* as his arm brushed hers, he was too good to be true. No man she'd ever known, including Clarence Nisbeth, whom she admired, had ever lifted a hand to help in the kitchen. Why, it just wasn't done. But it was so nice...

He glanced past her toward the window. "It's still snowing."

She pulled in a quiet breath. Translated, that undoubtedly meant she wasn't going home today, either. To her surprise, she realized she wasn't unhappy about it.

"It's about six weeks until Christmas," she began. "Do you and Joey celebrate it?"

He gave her a strange look. "Of course. Why wouldn't we?"

"Oh," she mumbled, embarrassed, "no reason. I just thought, I mean, your breakfast prayer was so—"

"I think it's important for Joey to remember his mother's culture as well as mine, which is the one he's being pushed into."

Eve glanced away. "I've heard...nothing about you and Joey," she began.

Snorting softly, he turned down the kerosene lamp on the table. "That surprises me. I was sure that you, like everyone else in this community, knew all about me."

The way he said it brought a tingling to the base of her neck. "Is there something else to know, other than that you married an Indian woman?"

He stood across the table from her, the low lamp light casting macabre shadows across his face. "I nearly killed my own brother because he murdered my wife."

Chapter Three

E ve leaned against the table, forcing her rubbery legs to hold her. "Your...brother murdered your wife?"

"Yes. And I nearly killed him for it. Now, are you anxious to leave? Doesn't it frighten you just a little to be in the same room with a man who could have murdered his own brother?"

It was as if he were baiting her, wanting her to be afraid, taunting her. "But... but you didn't." She held onto the back of a chair and studied him, hiding the internal panic he had so easily riled. "You're trying to scare me."

He gave her a sultry smile. "You mean I haven't succeeded?"

She let out a shaky breath and gave him a tremulous smile. "Oh, I wouldn't say that."

"Then, why aren't you screaming and running for the door?"

When she reached up to repair her hairdo, her fingers shook. She hoped he wouldn't notice. "I seldom do what's expected of me," she said with more bravado than she felt.

She removed the pins from her hair and splayed her fingers through the heavy mass that fell over her shoulder. She wanted to know more about him, but asking meant revealing her uncertainty, and she was stubborn enough not to want to show it.

Her fingers met tangles, and she frowned. It was bad enough she'd had to sleep in her clothes in a strange bed, but worse that she had no toiletries with her.

"Here. You can use this if you want to."

She glanced up to find him standing beside her, a brush in his hand. Nodding her thanks, she took it gratefully and pulled it through her hair.

A blast of cold air rushed into the room as Joey entered. He didn't speak for so long, Eve became concerned, fearing something was wrong. She glanced at him as he stood by the door, his wide eyes riveted on her.

Alarmed, she asked, "Is something wrong, Joey?"

He continued to stare at her as he stepped into the room and removed his jacket. Reaching out toward the peg on the wall, he attempted to hang his jacket on the hook by the door. It fell to the floor in a heap. "Holy smoke," he whispered, still staring at her. "She's really got angel hair, don't she, Pa?"

Her gaze swung to the boy's father, who was staring at her as well. The brief look of agony on his face disappeared, replaced by a cold, hard stare. He was silent.

"Your hair," Joey said, still mesmerized.

Eve looked away and began weaving her hair into a braid, finding the task difficult to do with such nervous fingers.

"Pa read me stories about Christmas angels. All the

while, I imagined them with hair like yours. Can't you leave it down?"

She gave him an anxious laugh, aware that although his father hadn't said a word, he hadn't taken his eyes off her, either. As she coiled the braid at the back of her head, she answered. "Now, how practical would that be? After all, you wouldn't want to catch fire while we're baking cookies, would you?"

His eyes brightened even more, and he grinned. "Cookies? Real cookies?"

Eve laughed, still aware of Sam standing quietly across from her. "Are there any other kind?" She turned to him. "Do you have flour and sugar?"

He led her to the small pantry.

Sam stayed out of their way. He couldn't stand to be close; it hurt like hell. Why she'd stumbled into their lives, he couldn't imagine. He knew Joey missed his mother's gentle touch. Maybe this was heaven's way of telling him the boy needed it.

Sam knew better. he and Joey were meant to go it alone. Sam's allegiance to the Indian community and his love for his half-breed son meant that for as long as they lived among the Whites, white women would cut a wide path around them. Hell, shortly after he and Joey had moved north, Sam had met a woman who'd showed immediate interest in him—until she saw Joey. And that hadn't been the first time.

Now, as he watched the angel-haired woman mix up

cookies with his son, he knew it would be the last. Baking cookies was one thing; Getting involved was another.

He sensed her pride and strength, though. What had he been thinking, blurting out that he nearly killed his brother? Not that it wasn't true, but he shouldn't have scared her like that. Maybe he just wanted to get rid of her. Maybe, in some idiotic way, he was afraid of her...

He swore again. He knew why he'd done it. He'd felt the attraction. But he couldn't afford to let thoughts of her linger, for never mind his own pain, there was Joey's to think about. Joey was drawn to any woman who'd bake him a batch of cookies, but this woman didn't belong with them, and tomorrow she'd be gone. And good riddance.

Sam almost wanted to drag her away from his son, to tell her to quit toying with him. But the force that prevented him from doing so was stronger. Watching Joey with her gave him pleasure, but not nearly as much pleasure as just watching her.

The delicious smell of ginger and molasses cookies filled the cabin. Joey stood on a stool beside the woman, rolling dough into walnut sized balls. They were talking and laughing together, and Sam wanted to bottle the scene before him and keep it forever. He knew there would be bleak days, weeks and years ahead when he'd want to remember things just as they were today.

"Hey, Pa! The cookies are ready. Here," Joey said, blowing on the hot molasses treat as he flipped it from one hand to the other. "Try one."

Sam wanted to say no, but his mouth watered. The cookie was big, round and flat and sprinkled with sugar. He bit into it and nearly groaned out loud. He closed his eyes, memories of his childhood flashing before him. He felt an ache deep inside a place he'd kept carefully protected.

When he opened his eyes, he found a cup of coffee and a plate of cookies sitting on the table before him.

No. Don't cave in. Don't let this happen. Don't dream of things that can never be. They'll bring you pain, Sammy-boy, nothing but pain.

But even as his mind warned him of the consequences, Sam took another cookie from the plate and devoured it, washing it down with a cup of excellent coffee.

As he nibbled a third cookie, he watched the woman work. She was at home in the kitchen and seemed to enjoy it. All right, So what? Sated now, he steeled himself against his feelings for her and all of what she could mean in his life. Cookies were one thing. At least she hadn't made bread. The one thing he couldn't fight against in the whole damn world was the taste of bread, fresh from the oven, slathered with creamy butter.

Joey rushed up to him, his eyes shining. "Pa! Guess what? Miss Engels is gonna bake us some bread!"

Sam tightened his jaw and stifled a groan.

For Eve, the day flew by. Thankfully. By busying herself in the kitchen, she didn't have to think about the man who watched her every move from somewhere behind her. As she worked, she found herself surprised that he'd even had the fixings for any baked goods. By evening, besides a batch of molasses cookies and freshly baked bread, she had a pot of stew bubbling over the fire.

And Joey... what a charming child he was. A thought had begun to form in her busy brain. She would approach the father before saying anything about it to Joey, just in case he didn't approve.

She turned as Sam Prescott entered the room from outside. Their gazes locked briefly before he turned away. "Supper is almost ready," she said, aware of the flutter of excitement his presence caused her. "Where's Joey?"

Sam hung his jacket on a hook and crossed to the washstand. "He'll be along."

She hovered behind him, watching him scrub his hands and splash water over his face. Now was as good a time as any. "I've been thinking—"

"Most women think too much," he interrupted as he dragged a towel across his face.

Mildly stung, she lifted her fist to her hips. "And every man alive thinks he's the biggest toad in the puddle. Now, may I continue?"

A smile lifted one corner of his mouth. "I doubt I could stop you."

Pulling in a satisfied breath she said, "If the school board won't allow Joey to attend school, at least for now," she said, certain she could do something about that, "then I think you should consider letting me come here to tutor him."

Sam continued wiping his hands on the towel, long after Eve was certain they were dry. "Why would you want to do that?"

"Because he's a delightful child and very bright. It would be tragic if he weren't allowed to learn to read and write."

"And how do you know he can't?" The question was defensive.

"Because he told me so," she answered tartly. "I just hope your stubborn pride won't stop you from consenting to my suggestion."

He studied her for a long, quiet minute before turning to hang the towel on the peg by the mirror. "And how often will you come to teach him?"

Eve straightened the silverware besides the plates, removed the kerosene lamp from the table and replaced it with a candle. "I'd like to come three afternoons a week. We can see how it goes from there." She held her breath as she waited for his answer.

"And I suppose you'll come in and make a mess of my kitchen each time."

Eve gasped. "A mess of your—" She clamped her mouth shut before she said something she might regret. It didn't help. "Please believe me, Mr. Prescott," she said with a sweet-tart smile, "I hope you live forever on hard tack and pig swill."

He nodded briskly. "As long as we understand each other."

"Fine. I'll begin tonight."

"Tonight?" He turned as Joey came in through the door, a rush of frigid air preceding him. Chancy was at his heels.

"Is there any reason why I shouldn't?"

He motioned Joey to the washstand. The boy's expression was proof that he was puzzled by the tension in the air.

"No, I guess not," Sam answered.

Moments later, they were all sitting at the table, eating their supper of stew and bread. Eve bit the insides of her cheeks as Joey once again enthused about her cooking. As she glanced at the intriguing, sullen man across from her, she couldn't help wondering why he was afraid of her. She would occasionally notice the warmth in his eyes as he watched Joey, but the minute he saw her watching him, his whole face changed. He would still show no emotion at all.

He just didn't want her around. That was obvious, but why? She didn't know a man in the world who would turn down home cooking, yet Sam Prescott had. Why, he'd almost made it sound revolting.

After the Evening meal was cleared away, the dishes done and Chancy fed, she sat with Joey, writing letters on the slate with chalk that she carried in her purse. His father sat nearby, pretending disinterest as he read a newspaper that was probably a month old.

After an hour, he looked up. "Joey, it's time for bed."

Joey didn't argue, but he looked at her, his eyes still filled with excitement. "How'm I doin', ma'am?"

Smiling down at him, she touched his cowlick. "Very well, Joey. Very well."

He grinned and nodded. "Well, goodnight, Miss Engels."

"Goodnight, Joey." She watched him pad to the ladder, her heart breaking when she noticed the holes in the toes of his wool stockings.

At the bottom of the ladder, he turned "You comin', Pa?"

"In a few minutes, son."

Appeased, he nodded and climbed to the loft.

Visions of bedtime brought Eve discomfort. She'd kept busy all day, able to keep her thoughts of Sam Prescott at bay, even though he was always close by. Despite his reti-cence, he fascinated her.

"I should be able to take you home tomorrow."

She realized that no one knew where she was, and although she wasn't accustomed to having anyone worry about her, no doubt Cora Nisbeth would. "The Nisbeth's are probably worried."

"That's where you live?"

She nodded. "You'll probably be glad to get rid of me and go back to your normal routine." When he didn't deny it, she felt a foolish stab of disappointment.

"How can I pay you for what you're doing for Joey?"

Frowning, she crossed to where he sat and dropped into the chair opposite him. "Pay me? Why, nothing. It's part of my job."

He looked away, appearing to study the fire. "No one does something for people like us for nothing."

She stiffened. "People like you. What's that supposed to mean?"

He folded the newspaper roughly, tossing it aside as he stood. "You know exactly what I mean."

Oh, yes, she knew. He was feeling sorry for himself. "You can't tell me you didn't know how people would react when they learned that you married an Indian. Certainly, you've come to terms with all of that, Mr. Prescott."

"I married an Indian because I fell in love with her. It wasn't until Joey was born that I realized what bigots my own people were."

She noted the sadness that cut into his features. Why was it so easy for some people to hurt others? It seemed that if a person were different, others coped with their lack of understanding by making fun of them and talking about them behind their backs. It was cruel, especially if a child was involved.

"It's been hard for you, hasn't it?"

He's strode to the ladder. "Yes, it's been hard. But we don't need your pity, ma'am."

She frowned as he retreated up the ladder. No, he didn't think he needed anything. But she wondered if he ever stopped to think of what Joey needed. She sensed that there was still a sad little boy inside Sam's big, hard body that felt rejected by his own people.

She watched him disappear into the loft, then made her way to the bed. She'd been in her clothes for two days, and she couldn't stand to sleep in them another night. Her corset dug into her ribs, and she felt sticky all over, despite the cool night air.

Eyeing the loft again to make sure Sam was up there to stay, she peeled off her clothes, leaving on only her chemise and drawers, then crawled into bed. As she shivered under the covers, she looked at the fireplace. The fire was almost out. He'd forgotten to bank it.

She flung the covers back and left the bed, padding quietly to the wood box. She lifted a heavy wood chunk and dumped it into the grate, where it appeared to smother the remaining embers. Spying the poker that rested against the wall, she grabbed it and began jabbing at the log.

"Here, I'll do that."

His voice made her jump, and she turned toward him, the poker still in her fist. Unable to look him in the eyes, she allowed her gaze to drop down to the neck of his long underwear, which was open to the middle of his chest. Dark hair curled there, clear up to the pulse that pounded at his throat and down across his hard, flat chest.

Automatically dropping her gaze lower, she saw that he'd either been in the process of removing his pants, or pulling them back on, for they weren't buttoned up all the way. They hung low on his hips, and even though he was fully covered by his underwear, it seemed indecent.

"Seen enough?"

She felt heat rush to her face as she quickly looked up at him. That maddening half smile and those sultry eyes made her look away. "You forgot to bank the fire."

He took the poker from her. His touch, though surely innocent, sent a spiral of heat into her belly.

"Having a woman around seems to have caused my good senses to take a holiday."

She stepped away yet stayed close to the fire. It was warm, yet she suddenly shivered. She really ought to scurry back to bed and—

He went past her to retrieve another wood chunk, giving her a quick glance as he did so. "Nice underwear."

Her flush deepened, and she crossed her arms over her chest. "I'm sorry, I'll go back to bed—"

"No," he rasped harshly. "Stay a minute."

Her heart thudded madly, and though all her good sense told her to bolt and run she stayed.

Once the fire was banked, he rested the poker against the wall and turned to her. His gaze raked over her, briefly stopping at places that automatically reacted. Like her breasts, which suddenly tingled, and her stomach, which quivered, and the place below...

"There's more danger for you here at this very minute than you'll ever know." His voice was a husky whisper.

She was quivering inside and couldn't speak. If she had, she would have told him she knew that. Still, she didn't move away.

Stepping close, he reached over and brought her thick rope of hair over her shoulder, cradling it in the palm of his hand. The backs of his finger rested against her breast, and she felt her nipples tighten beneath her chemise. She stood still, but inside she was shaking with the newness of her feelings.

He unbraided her hair, the rough edges of his fingers occasionally snagging it as he worked the hair loose. She forced herself to stand quietly before him. This was wrong; she knew it, but she didn't care. she'd been wildly curious about him from the beginning, and though he'd made every effort to show her he felt nothing, she sensed it wasn't true.

She glanced briefly at his face. His eyes were dark, but light from the fire made them smolder. She tried to control her breathing but noticed that he couldn't control his, either. She had a reckless urge to touch his jaw, to rub the backs of her fingers against his stubble.

Suddenly his fingers, which had been resting almost innocently against her breast, pressed against it. Her gaze shot to his again, and there was an unasked question in his eyes. Oh, sweet heaven, she should run. Scurry back to bed. But she didn't. She merely closed her eyes and waited.

Slowly, as though he had all the time in the world, his fingers left her hair and moved gently over the swell of her breast. Her nipples tensed further, pulling her breasts so tight she swore she could feel them harden. There was an ache down deep between her legs. It was as if she discovered an uncharted path from her breast to that secret place below.

He circled her breast with his fingers, then touched her pebbled nipple. She grasped for breath and stepped away, for had she not, she might have thrown herself at him, the feelings he'd stirred within her were so strong,

"Like I said," he murmured sarcastically, "you're in more danger now than you'll ever know."

Her eyes snapped open, and she saw the change that had come over him. He was no longer hungry; he merely wanted to hurt her but he hadn't. She hadn't known him very long, but she already felt she knew him well. Whenever he was afraid, he lashed out. It was his defense. And again, she realized that for some reason, he was afraid of her.

Without bothering to answer, she stumbled back to his bed, crawled under the covers and turned to face the wall. Not until she heard him climb the ladder to the loft did she let out the breath she was holding.

She lay there, studying the darkness, beginning to feel a kernel of shame uncoil inside her. How brazen she'd been! Had he tried to kiss her, she wouldn't have pushed him away.

Suddenly, she was elated to be leaving in the morning. Her heart told her one thing while her head fairly shouted another. Wisely, she listened to the scolding in her head. But it was still impossible to fall asleep.

Chapter Four

E ve stood at the Nisbeth parlor window and watched Sam Prescott drive away, the bells on the teams' bridle ringing in the cold morning air. As he'd predicted, the day had donned sunny and still, and he'd been able to bring her home in the sleigh. He'd insisted he would pick her up from school those afternoons she was to tutor Joey, and she hadn't been able to refuse, although she wasn't sure how it was going to look.

Now that she was home, her decision to tutor Joey didn't seem quite as sound as it had been when she made it. She didn't want to lose her job, but how could she live with herself if she didn't try to help the boy? He was very bright. That kind of child didn't come along every day.

Cora Nisbeth appeared beside her, put her arm around her and drew her close.

When Eve had arrived home, Cora had hugged her so tightly, she'd been nearly suffocated. "If I weren't so happy to see you, young lady, I'd spank you like a child," she'd scolded. "Do you realize how many people were looking for you? Lan' sakes, the most *awful* thoughts went through my head. I…I thought maybe you had frozen to death in a snowbank. Or worse yet, you could have been eaten by wolves." Cora pressed her fingers to her lips, but a quiet sob escaped anyway.

Eve felt awful. She didn't want people to worry about her. She wasn't used to it. Until the Nisbeths had come into her life, no one had really cared much about her. It was touching, and she felt like crying herself. Instead, she gave Cora a sisterly hug.

"I'm sorry you all worried about me, but I was lucky to find a place to wait out the storm." She sighed. "I'd heard about people losing their bearings in a blizzard. I just didn't think it would ever happen to me."

Cora clucked her tongue. "But of all places to be…"

"Oh, it wasn't so bad. Joey's a charming child. It just makes me want to spit when I think of the school board turning him away."

"You know how Clarence feels about Indians, Eve." Cora led her from the window to the sofa in front of the fire. "One doesn't lose one's only sister to the Indians without feeling bitter and angry."

Eve shivered and rubbed her arms. "Oh, that dreadful New Ulm massacre. I understand his grief, Cora, but why does he have to take it out on a child?"

Cora poured Eve a cup of coffee and pressed it into her hands. "The subject of Clarence's family is the least of your worries, dear. Even if I don't say anything about where you've been for the past two days, word will get around, and—"

"Cora," she interrupted, "I couldn't have left had I

wanted to. And Mr. Prescott was a perfect gentleman." More or less, she realized, but what had happened between them had been as much her fault has his. A pleasurable rush of goose flesh scampered over her arms.

"Still," Cora continued, unaware of Eve's thoughts, "people will talk And what about the new preacher?"

Eve was startled for a moment. "What about him?"

"You know he thinks of you so fondly," Cora reminded her.

Eve sighed, recalling the way the Reverand Adam Brewster's eyes focused on her so often in church. "Well, he hasn't come calling, has he?" she answered tartly.

"But everyone knows that just a little kindness from you would change his world."

It had entered her mind. After all, he was a good, kind man, pleasant looking, and bravely raising three children with the help of his sister after his wife's death. But she wasn't ready for such a commitment, even if he truly thought of her that way.

"It might be the best choice you will ever make," Cora said softly.

"I have other things to think about, Cora, and I'd best let it be known right now that I'm planning to tutor Joey Prescott three afternoons a week." She paused. "Isn't your niece Trudy going to work for the reverend now that his sister is ill?"

Cora waved her hand, dismissing it. "That has nothing to do with you."

"Why not? She's in a perfect position."

Cora frowned. "Trudy? But she's a widow, and much too old for him anyway."

Eve chuckled. "She's not that old. She can't be thirty."

"Well, he's probably not looking for a wife anyway," Cora presumed. "And you have just successfully avoided my response to that last bit of news. Tutor that boy? You must be out of your mind."

"Cora, I have to. It's part of my job, and nowhere in my contract does it say I can't tutor children in special circumstances on my own time."

She knew that Cora had been involved in writing up the terms of the contract. Now, she could sense her going over what she'd help compose.

"But we didn't imagine anything like this would happen," Cora argued weakly.

"Well, everyone respects you, Cora. If you don't make a big issue of it, no one else will, either."

Cora heaved a sigh. "It would almost be worth it to get the boy into school rather than having you traipse over there. Why, you'll be at his mercy, Eve, you'll—"

"Oh, Cora," Eve answered on a laugh. "Believe me, he isn't too thrilled about my coming over there. He made that perfectly clear. But he's a good father, no matter what any of you think, and he only wants what's best for his son."

Cora gently patted the area over her heart, as if warding off a swoon. It was a tactic Eve had discovered the woman used mostly when she wanted something from her husband.

Eve put her coffee cup down and stood. "Don't give me that faint hearted expression, Cora. Just be there with me if and when I have to face the school board."

Cora sighed and shook her head. "I'm afraid that under the circumstances, that will be sooner than you think. Clarence has called a meeting for tonight."

Eve's shoulders drooped. She wasn't looking forward to it. She hated confrontations, she always had. The only thing that gave her strength was to think ahead to the next afternoon, when she would see Sam Prescott again. In spite of the cold draft that whistled in under the door, she felt as though she'd captured a smoldering ember near her heart.

That evening, Eve faced the members of the school board in the Nisbeth parlor. Cora had started decorating for Christmas. Bittersweet berries, nested in the evergreen sprigs of the fragrant red cedar, bedecked the mantle.

Unfortunately, the festive warmth of the decorations didn't reach out and penetrate the people in the room. Henry Hassler sat stoically gazing at the fire, while his brother stared at Eve from behind steepled fingers.

Cora's fingers flew over her knitting. The needles clicking rhythmically. Now and then she glanced up at her husband, who examined Eve's contract. Suddenly he stood and dropped the contract on the desk.

"Well, it appears you're right, Eve."

She held her breath.

Clarence Nisbeth crossed to where she sat and studied her for a moment. The look on his face told Eve that he wasn't happy about admitting he was wrong. "We didn't provide for such an occurrence. Seems you can tutor the boy on your own time. Just see that it doesn't interfere with the work we've hired you for."

Eve nearly sagged with relief. "Of course it won't inter-fere. But it would be so much easier if he could just—"

"Eve," Cora interrupted quietly but firmly, "let it go."

Eve took a deep breath and leaned back in her chair. Yes, better to let it go—for now. But somehow, some way she would get Joey Prescott into her classroom.

Although Eve was nervous about her first session with Joey since they'd been snowbound, when she saw the Prescott sleigh coming toward the building, she bundled up in her warm clothes and carried the supplies she would need for Joey outside. Also stuffed deep in her valise were darning thread and a needle. The condition of Joey socks was shameful. She wouldn't bother to ask Sam Prescott if she could darn them; she'd just do it.

She saw that Sam was alone, and he didn't look happy. He really didn't want her help; she wished she knew why. Before she could even greet him, he started in on her.

"Joey and I don't need you interfering in our lives, Miss Engels. I heard about you begging to get Joey into school. We don't need pity or charity." As he assisted her into the sleigh and lifted the quilt over her knees, Eve noticed a muscle tighten in his jaw.

She ignored his reprimand. "Where's Joey?"

"He'll be there by the time we get home."

"Good. And I didn't beg," she said, answering his

rebuke. "But one way or another, I'll get him into school. Until then, I'll tutor him." She turned and glared at him. "I can't see why my decision should bother you. It's for Joey's own good."

He walked around the horses and pulled himself onto the seat beside her. As he slid beneath the quilt, Eve felt a flutter of pleasure. It seems so... intimate. She fought the memory of their night together in front of the fire.

Sam flipped the reins over the team, and the horses started down the snowy path, bells jingling. "We can fight our own battles."

"And it certainly appears that you've done a fine job," she answered with a measure of sarcasm.

Ignoring her tone, he said, "They want my land for their new schoolhouse. That's my ace in the hole to finally get Joey into school. I don't need you."

She turned and studied him, feeling a quivering in her stomach as she realized that he was, in truth, as compelling as she'd remembered. The cold winter air had nipped his cheeks, rendering them apple red beneath his dark stubble. His nose, so straight, seemed chiseled from granite. His cheekbones were high and sharply defined.

"Unless someone else gives them a better offer," she said, then looked away, wishing she could find him uninteresting. "Isn't there some land across the lake from the community building?"

He was silent for a moment, then answered. "Yes. But it belongs to old man Torkelson. He refuses to sell. Seems he wants to lay in a corn crop there."

Eve nodded. Jeremiah Torkelson and his wife, Mavis, were loners, too. Eve didn't think she'd ever seen Mavis in town, or anywhere else, for that matter. As far as she knew, they'd never had children, and Jeremiah wasn't too keen on having the schoolhouse built on his land, even if it meant getting paid for it.

Eve was suddenly aware that her hand had landed inadvertently on Sam's thigh beneath the quilt. Their gazes met, and she removed her hand and quickly looked away. "I... I hope you're right. If there's anything I can do to convince them—"

"Like I said, Miss Engels," he interrupted, "don't go meddling in my affairs. The last thing I need is some fool woman trying to fight my battles."

Eve held her tongue, but she was seething inside. *Men.* They were so...so stubborn. Finally, after stewing for a good minute, she said, "If you would present yourself to the community in a friendlier manner, maybe they'd be more obliging to you."

He snorted. "Yeah, like that would do any good."

"Well, it couldn't hurt. Don't you see what you're doing? You're acting exactly the way they expect you to."

He shot her a quick, angry glance that held underlying interest. "What do you mean?"

She pulled in a breath of frigid air, then watched it cloud before her as she exhaled. "I mean, because you lived with the Indians for so many years, people just figure you're one of them. You're on their side, no matter what. In essence," she added, "you're a traitor."

"Damn it! I'm not a traitor. Why can't they understand that?"

She shrugged. "How can they? You moved here with Joey and became a recluse. You don't mingle with any of the people in town. You avoid conversations with everyone. You bought land that no one thought you could afford, being an Indian lover and all—"

"Aw, hell," he interrupted again. "You're no better than the rest of them."

"But don't you see? That's not me saying those things. It's everyone who's ever seen you ride sullenly into town, go wordlessly about your business, then slink back to your farm. Just by your actions you've proven that you're exactly what they thought you would be."

He sat quietly beside her as if digesting what she'd said. "I don't see what I can do to change their minds. "

"You could start smiling...just a little." She gave him a sidelong glance and felt a rush of delight when he smiled— against his will, no doubt. "See? Now, the next time you go into town, smile at the merchants. Tip your hat at the ladies. Let them know you're human and pleasant and not some crazy hermit."

He snorted again. "I can't do that."

Surprised, she looked at him. "And why not?"

He squirmed on the seat, unconsciously touching Eve's hip. She briefly closed her eyes as the pleasure threaded through her.

"Because it's just not something I could do."

"Then I suggest you work at it." She touched his knee again, this time on purpose, and didn't pull her hand away. They sat quietly, the air filled with an unusual tension. Eve's heart pounded hard, for she knew she was being forward, but she felt a recklessness that was new to her, and she didn't care.

Chapter Five

Their afternoon session went well. Because she was so pleased with Joey's progress, she told him that the next time she came, she'd tell him the story of *The Christmas Cuckoo*. Eve had made the story into a play and the children would act it out for their parents at the Christmas pageant.

Now, as she darned the socks Joey had brought her, she felt him staring at her from across the table.

"Miss Engels?"

"Yes, Joey?" she answered with a smile.

"You stayin' for supper?"

Her heart nearly broke, supplication was written all over his face, but she forced herself to stay unaffected. "I'm sure your father has something planned." Joey's glance shot toward the door. "Aw, we'll prob'ly just have tater hash."

Eve couldn't suppress a smile. "Tater' hash? Doesn't sound too exciting I will admit," Joey sighed and stared at the fire. "Nothin's been as good as what you made, Miss Engels. All the cookies are gone, and I think Pa ate the last of the bread yesterday. And we ain't … I mean, we haven't had nothin' as good as that stew you made."

Eve's determination not to interfere in their daily routine had already been broken since she was darning socks. What harm would it do to make them a bite of dinner? "All right. What are you hungry for, Joey?"

Joey sighed and gave her a blissful smile. "Pa and I caught some fish through the ice on the lake yesterday. How 'bout if we have them?"

"Hmmm. Did you clean them?"

"Yep. All cleaned and ready to fry."

Eve put her darning down on the floor beside the chair. "All right. You get the fish, and I'll do the rest."

Sam frowned as he entered the cabin. The lingering smell of batter-fried fish and onions filled the room, and he let out a quiet curse.

After hanging up his jacket, he removed his boots and stepped into the room. The little busybody stood over the stove, stirring something in a skillet. Freshly baked biscuits were heaped on a plate.

The table was set for three.

"Pa! Guess what we're havin' for supper."

Sam gave Joey a dark look, but the boy was too engrossed in food to notice. "Hard tack and pig swill?"

Eve turned from the stove and gave him a little smile. "That would serve you right, wouldn't it?" He lifted an eyebrow at her but said nothing.

Joey, oblivious to their repartee, answered. "Heck, no,

Pa. We're havin' fried fish, creamed taters with onions and peas and fresh biscuits!"

Eve lifted the skillet and dumped the potato mixture into a bowl. "I'm surprised at the treasures you have in your pantry, Mr. Prescott. Why, I couldn't believe you actually had some peas. Don't tell me you do your own canning?"

"I got them from Mavis Torkelson last fall," he muttered.

She gave him a look of dry surprise. "Oh, you do get along with someone, then?"

He wanted to give her a sarcastic answer, but suddenly he couldn't think of one.

"'Hurry and wash up, Pa. I'm hungrier than a bear."

With a mixture of reluctance and pleasure, Sam cleaned up for supper, his stomach growling in anticipation.

The meal was filled with Joey's chatter about his recent encounter with some of the boys from Eve's class at school. Apparently, they all met down by the lake.

"I hope none of you boys are foolish enough to walk out onto the lake. It might be frozen, but it could still be dangerous," Sam said.

"I know that, Pa. But that Ernie Nisbeth. He pretends he's not afraid of nothin'. 'He's out on the lake, darin' everyone else to join him. He's a real skunk."

"A skunk?"' Eve bit into a biscuit, relieved they were light and fluffy.

"He's kinda mean but I don't think he wants to be all the time. He just is, like he can't do nothin' about it."

Eve thought about it. Yes, Ernest was probably the most troublesome child she had in the classroom, and she couldn't understand it because his parents were genuinely fine people who treated all their children fairly. It was almost as if Ernest had come from a bad seed.

"What did you and the boys talk about?"

Joey chewed on a piece of fish, then looked at his father. "Well, I told them I could write Indian sign language."

Eve put down her fork. "You can? Why, I think that's wonderful, Joey."

Joey looked at his father again, then shrugged. "Yeah, but Ernie didn't believe me. Said I was just makin' it all up and that anybody could make stick pictures in the snow."

Eve wanted to throttle Ernest. "Well, don't let him bother you, Joey. The other boys are nice, aren't they?"

He shrugged again. "Sometimes. But not when they're with Ernie."

Sam cleared his throat and stood. "It's time for me to take you home, Miss Engels."

Eve glanced at the cluttered table. "Oh, but the dishes—"

"Joey will tend to those."

Eve sighed. Sam wanted her gone.

"When you comin' again, ma'am?" Joey asked.

Eve allowed Sam to help her with her coat. "I'll be here on Wednesday, and you'll learn about *The Christmas Cuckoo*."

Joey grinned and nodded, but continued to stare at her, clearly wanting to say something else.

"Yes, Joey, what is it?"

He gave his father a quick glance, ignoring the stern look, then asked, "Do you s'pose we can bake some more of them cookies?!"

Eve could feel Sam's hands tense on her shoulders. She remembered how little he wanted her around, but she refused to make up some silly excuse just for him. She had no reason to disappoint Joey.

"How about if we start baking some Christmas things?"

He gave her a puzzled look. "Christmas things?"

"Yes, like sweet Christmas bread with fruit and nuts, cookies with butter and sugar frosting, apple pie—"

"Oh, yes, ma'am," he said with a wide grin. "I'd like that just fine."

"All right, Joey. I'll see you on Wednesday, then." She felt Sam pushing her toward the door. Over her shoulder, she called, "Don't forget to study those letters!"

"I won't! I won't forget, ma'am!"

Sam took her arm and pulled her roughly toward the waiting sleigh. "I don't want you doing this," he said gruffly.

She settled onto the bench and pulled the quilt over her knees. When he was seated close beside her, their bodies touching to generate warmth, she asked, "Why is it so hard for you to let me do things for him?"

He was silent for a time. The only sound in the crisp, cold air was the jingling of the sleigh bells attached to the harness. "Because in the end, he'll only be disappointed."

Frowning, Eve digested his words. "I'd never disappoint him, Sam."

He cursed under his breath. "You just don't get it, do you?"

His words were harsh. Cold. And they hurt. "I guess I'm just too stupid to understand how cooking a few meals and baking cookies for a delightful little boy could possibly disappoint him. Why don't you explain it to me?"

He cursed again. "For a woman, you talk pretty boldly."

"I'm not trying to be bold, Mr. Prescott," she retorted

angrily. "I'm just trying to understand what you have against me."

"Ah, hell. It's not against you, personally. It's just that…" He took a deep breath. "All right, I'll say it right out. After you have your fun playing house, cooking and baking for my boy, you'll get tired of it soon enough. Then what? It's better if Joey doesn't get used to such stuff. It's better if…if you just let us be."

She should have been angry at his words. Instead, they made her want to cry. Not for herself but for Joey. Her eyes filled and her throat closed. "Everyone deserves a little pleasure in life, Sam. Especially little boys like Joey who have so many more hurdles to jump than a white child. No one, not even a well-meaning father, should prevent him from having whatever pleasures are available to him."

They rode the rest of the way in silence. Eve knew he was trying to push her away. As for Joey, why, she'd never just up and leave him. They were friends. She could understand why Sam would be upset if she were the kind of person who would garner Joey's friendship, then drop him when she got bored, but she wasn't like that.

She had a special feeling for Sam, too, but the feeling wasn't reciprocated. Something deep inside her wished it would be, but wishing never made anything happen.

Cora met her at the door, stern-faced. "It's about time you got home."

Eve removed her boots, leaving them just inside the door before stepping into the room. "It's not that late." She feigned nonchalance, knowing that Cora had probably held supper for her.

"I suppose you've eaten?"

"Well, I could hardly deny the boy supper, Cora."

Cora followed her up the stairs to her room. "Is this going to be an ongoing thing? Eating supper with them?"

Eve was tired. School was hard enough, since this would be her first Christmas pageant, and she wanted to do it right. Then, spending another few hours tutoring Joey made for a very long day. Not that she'd have it any other way. It was just that she wanted the holiday to be perfect, both at school and for Joey. Her seventeen Christmases in the orphanage had been bleak. She had a lot to make up for.

The schoolchildren were so excited about Christmas. Although they gladly memorized the songs and their parts for the play and delighted in making decorations for the walls and windows, they were still a handful. Even pesky Ernest was well behaved at this time of year, but that didn't make him any less rambunctious.

"Well? Are you always going to eat with them?" Cora asked again.

"Oh, I don't know. Probably. I can't say no to little Joey. He…he seems to need some softness in his life, and as long as he wants something from me that I can give, I don't see any reason not to. And whatever Sam thinks—"

"*Sam*? Now it's Sam?" Cora interrupted plaintively. "I don't believe this, Eve. You're calling that man by his first name. It's…well, it's just not proper."

Eve closed her eyes and rubbed her neck. "Cora, you're making too much of it. It's nothing, believe me. He still calls me 'ma'am.' Now, does that satisfy you?" She unbuttoned her dress, stepped out of it and hung it in the wardrobe.

"Oh, I just worry so about you, dear. When I first saw you that day we stopped at the orphanage to deliver that load of fresh vegetables, my heart went out to you. You were the most beautiful young thing I'd ever seen. And so polite. 'Clarence,' I said, 'can't we take her home with us?! But Clarence said it would be far better for you to stay there and attend normal school in St. Paul. The nuns were grateful we wanted to pay for your education, and we were happy to do it. Now, you're like my own daughter. I don't want to see you hurt, dear."

Eve felt a measure of guilt. Clarence and Cora Nisbeth were the first real family she'd ever had. And they'd made her dream of becoming a teacher come true. She didn't want to hurt them, but she couldn't explain exactly what she was feeling for Joey. She just knew she couldn't abandon him.

And Sam… She wasn't sure what she felt for him, either, but whatever it was, she didn't want it to stop. That was a frightening realization.

She went over and gave Cora a hug. "You know I'll never be able to repay you and Clarence for what you've done for me. But I don't want you to worry about me. That's a terrible responsibility for you."

Cora watched as Eve folded her underthings and carefully laid them across a chair. "I just don't want you to be hurt, dear. Not by anyone, and that includes the people in this community once they hear what you're doing."

Eve felt a nudge of exasperation. As she unbraided her hair, she couldn't keep from saying, "Is it because the man is a widower with a half-breed child? I can't help but wonder how much different their reaction might be if Joey were white."

Cora took the brush from Eve and pulled it through her long, thick hair. It had become a ritual; Cora had always told her she had pretty hair. "Angel hair," she called it. Eve smiled, remembering that Joey had called it that, too.

"I won't deny that it would make a difference," Cora said. "We all just want you to be happy and—"

"And you don't think I can be happy with a man who has slept with an Indian woman."

Cora gasped and brought her hand over her heart. "Eve Engels, don't talk so boldly. It's not a bit ladylike, and you know it."

Eve didn't want to argue. No one understood what she was feeling, and they would never understand even if she tried to explain. She'd had her share of suitors, but no man she'd ever known had made her feel like Sam Prescott did. He could be the devil himself, and it wouldn't matter. For better or worse, she was drawn to him.

"I'm sorry, Cora, I didn't mean to offend you. I'm just tired, I guess."

Cora pressed her shoulders. "Of course you are, dear. I'll leave you."

Eve watched Cora quietly close the door behind her. She heard the clock on the mantel in the parlor chime nine times. After turning out her lamp, she climbed into bed, comforted by the familiarity, yet remembering the distinctly male scents from Sam's bedding. Trying to recapture the sensation, she drifted into a restful sleep.

Chapter Six

Although it was very early to do so, the children had decorated the insides of the windows with brightly colored green wreaths and red bows. Mother Nature had decorated the outside, adorning each pane with frost. The bright, cold sun spattered the frost with brilliance, often creating colorful prisms of light.

Inside, color suffused every available wall space, too. Christmas trees and manger scenes and children skating on a frozen lake papered the walls like a seasonal mosaic. Strings of threaded popcorn were draped over the door and windows, and bittersweet berries nested in evergreen branches.

The preacher, Reverend Brewster, didn't seem to mind that he had to share the room. Eve thought he was probably used to it, although she began to think he stayed around because of her. His gaze followed her frequently when he lifted his head from his work.

The community building was put to a variety of uses all year long; people gathered to hear traveling speakers and musicians and to enjoy basket socials. Why, last summer they had even held a pig auction. Naturally, the pigs stayed outside.

Eve could tell that the Reverend Brewster truly loved children, because he often stopped by to admire their drawings and listen to their Christmas recitations. He was a pleasant man of medium stature with light curls that clung softly to his head. Eve wondered about his youngsters, who were still too young to attend school. She also was curious about how Trudy was getting along.

The older boys had hauled in a Christmas tree. It was a graceful red cedar, and the children couldn't wait to put on the candles and light them. Eve had to remind them that they would be lit only at the Christmas program, over a week away, then again on Christmas Eve, for the church service. They all groaned good-naturedly.

After the children were dismissed, Eve noticed that the reverend was still at his desk at the back of the room. She took her coat off the hook by the door and was going to bid him a good day when he called out to her.

"Miss Engels? Can I have a moment?"

She placed her coat over the back of a chair and went to where he sat. "What is it?"

He didn't look at her but seemed dreadfully interested in the lump of glass he used for a paperweight. "Please, would you mind taking a seat?"

Concern washed over her as she sat in the chair in front of him, waiting for him to continue.

He sighed. "Miss Engels, it has come to my attention that...that you have been spending time, unescorted, with one of our, well...now understand that I do not have anything against Mr. Prescott. I, myself, have lived among the tribes and have great respect for them.

"But, when the church council bids me do something, it is in my contract to do so."

Eve's blood began to boil. Oh, those contracts! "And what have they told you I must do?"

He once again turned the paperweight round and round on the desk. "You must know how this looks, and what damage it will do." He looked up, obviously uncomfortable. "Your reputation is at stake here. You are a lovely young woman and I'd—"

"I believe my reputation is my business, and no one else's."

For the first time, he openly studied her. "Your job could be at stake,"

A sudden bolt of fear rattled her. "But my contract says nothing about the company I keep, and I only have to abide Mr. Prescott because I'm tutoring his son."

"Then perhaps it would be best if Sam Prescott dropped his son off here, after school hours."

She nearly snorted. "Oh, that makes perfect sense, doesn't it? Mr. Prescott is so anxious to have me out of his hair that he would find it a perfect time to discontinue Joey's education."

Reverend Prescott frowned. "You mean he wouldn't do this for his son?"

"No, he would not."

"I see. Well, I hope you come to the right decision."

Eve stood and put on her coat, hat and gloves, then left the building realizing that the reverend was no longer apt to court her!

Over the past weekend, Eve had visited the homes of her students. It was important for all the parents to know that they weren't to bring gifts for their children to the Christmas program. Since only a few families could afford it, it was better if no one did. Gifts for only a few would make the others unhappy.

She also realized that her trips to tutor Joey had spread like, well wildfire. No parent said anything, but some looked at her strangely.

She knew that Clarence had purchased a barrel of apples and was going to hand out one to each child that evening. It was a wonderful gesture, but every family couldn't be expected to do the same. And Eve and Cora and Trudy planned to bake fresh gingerbread cookies, decorating them with frosting as a special treat for each child.

Eve wasn't sure, but she thought that perhaps other mothers would do something for each child, too. On the surface, all things pointed to a successful Christmas program.

On the surface. But each time she thought about Sam and Joey, excluded from the community, all her Christmas spirit fled.

While she waited for Sam to pick her up after school, she trudged through the snow to the stand of cedars that stood behind the church. She was looking for boughs to decorate

Sam and Joey's cabin. She already had popping corn in her valise so they could pop it and string it for decoration.

A clump of bittersweet berries caught her eye, and she pulled it off and gently put it in her pocket. Perhaps Joey knew where they could find some more.

Hearing the sound of Sam's sleigh, she hurried to the road and waved as he drove up. Joey was with him, and he gave her a wide, happy smile. Sam appeared solemn. She felt immediate concern. After the meeting with the reverend, she didn't know what to expect from anyone.

She climbed in, and Joey made room for her between him and his father. After greeting him warmly, she turned to Sam.

"Aren't you feeling well?"

"I'm fine."

Obviously, he was in one of his stoic moods. She turned to Joey. "We have so much to do after your lessons today, Joey. I was wondering if you knew where there are any bittersweet berries."

"Sure do," he answered with enthusiasm. "What're you gonna make with 'em? Somethin' to eat?"

She laughed gaily. "Is that all you ever think about?"

He grinned back. "It is ever since you started comin' over, Miss Engels."

She nudged his shoulder. "We have to start decorating the cabin for Christmas." She held up her valise. "Guess what I have in here?"

"Is it somethin' to eat?"

She laughed again. "Yes and no. I mean, you can eat it, but you can also use it for decorations."

'Well, what is it?"

She shook her head. "I told you to guess. I'm not going to make it easy for you." He made a playful lunge for her valise, causing her to pull it away. She fell against Sam. When she turned to look at him, she stopped laughing. He truly looked ill.

Once they reached the cabin, she became so engrossed in Joey's lessons, she temporarily forgot about Sam's pique. When the lessons were done, she and Joey popped the corm she'd brought.

Eve heaped it high in a bowl on the table. She reached into her valise and pulled out a small sewing kit. As she threaded a needle for Joey, she caught him stuffing the popcorn into his mouth.

She laughed softly. "At that rate, there won't be any left to string."

Joey tried to grin, but his cheeks were puffed out like a squirrel's. "Me'n Chancy love popcorn," he said around his mouthful.

Eve glanced at the dog, who had been allowed inside more and more often since she'd started coming over and discovered him pushing some popcorn around on the hearth with his nose. "Oh, Joey. Chancy's not eating it. He's playing with it."

"Aw, he'll eat it pretty soon. Chancy'll eat anything," he answered, swallowing what he had in his mouth. "Once he ate a mouse; I saw him. An' there was that time he dragged home a dead skunk—"

That's enough, Joey," Sam interrupted.

Shuddering, Eve tossed Sam a grateful, although weak smile, trying not to remember how often she'd allowed Chancy to lick her face. "Well," she said, turning back to her task, "this is what we do." She showed Joey the threaded needle and carefully pushed it through a few pieces of popcorn, then a bittersweet berry, alternating them that way until she had a gay red and white chain. She showed him how to knot the ends when he was done.

Joey worked carefully, his face pinched in concentration. "Pa? You gonna help?"

His father glanced up from his newspaper, then buried his face in it again. "You're doing fine, Joey." Eve felt a stab of disappointment. It would be so good for all of them to do this together, but she couldn't force him to participate. She sighed. So much for her silly dreams. She should know better.

When Joey ran out of the berries Eve had brought, he bundled up and left the cabin with Chancy to find some more. Eve turned her attention back to the fresh, hot bread she'd just taken from the oven. She wiped the top of the loaf with butter, then looked at Sam. He was sitting at the table staring at her, his expression dour.

"Sam, I know you don't feel well. You've hardly said a word since you picked me up."

He continued to stare at her. "You're doing this on purpose, aren't you?"

His tone startled her. "What do you mean?"

"You know damn well what I mean."

Bravely ignoring his words, Eve walked around to where he sat and touched his forehead. He flinched, pulling her hand away. He didn't release her wrist.

She swallowed hard. "I…thought you might be running a fever…"

"I am, dammit, but not where you think."

She stared at him, his words both frightening and thrilling her. "That...that's hardly the thing to say..."

His grip tightened, and he pulled her to him, his face dangerously close to her breasts. "You're driving me crazy."

The sound of his voice uttered so angrily made her knees buckle. She tried to pull her arm away. He didn't release it. Instead, he stood and dragged her close.

"I'm not... I mean, I haven't..." Lord, she didn't know what she meant. Her heart felt all fluttery inside her chest. She studied his face. There was a handsome cleft in his chin beneath his stubble. His eyebrows were sharply defined, and his thick lashes fringed his hauntingly beautiful eyes.

He still clutched her wrist but put it behind her back, bringing her even closer. Excitement at his nearness won out over her fear. She was mesmerized by his touch, his dark, brooding looks. He made her weak. She relaxed against him and felt rather than heard his sharp intake of breath. Her gaze moved slowly to where their bodies touched, and she suddenly understood his reaction. Her breasts were flat against his chest.

A tingling, stinging sensation radiated through her, making her nipples hard and tight. It was exactly the same feeling she'd had when he'd touched her that night in front of the fire. Slowly she moved her gaze back to his face. A muscle twitched in his jaw. His breathing became the slightest bit erratic, and his eyes focused on her mouth.

Before she knew what was happening, he was kissing her —hard, angry kisses that were undoubtedly intended to punish. She'd never been kissed like this before.

Something sweet and warm erupted inside her, deep down between her legs, and she threw her free arm around him, answering his violent response. He forced his way into her mouth, his tongue sparring with hers. Releasing her arm, he brought his hands to her head, holding her as he ravaged her.

Eve felt a wild, uninhibited response to his kiss and found herself clutching him tightly. She heard him groan into her mouth and his touch softened; their mouths clung. His hands left her hair and roamed over her back. He lifted her slightly, pressing her close, and she felt the hard ridge beneath his jeans. The sensation heated her blood, and it pounded through her veins, expanding in her abdomen; making her want something she hadn't known existed.

Abruptly, he lowered her feet to the floor without letting her go. "That shouldn't have happened." His voice was harsh, husky,

She could barely stand; her legs felt like quivering aspen twigs. Oh, had she known what two people could feel... And whether he wanted to admit it or not, he felt something powerful for her, too.

Braving his mood, she reached up and touched his chin. He gripped her fingers and held them while he pierced her with his dark gaze,

"What in the hell do you want from us?"

"W-want from you?" That quivering little voice was actually hers.

"It's a simple enough question," he answered, his voice as gritty as sandpaper.

"I care about you and Joey. I—" She stopped, knowing she was about to tell Sam she was falling in love with him. But she couldn't say it; she could hardly believe it herself.

Instead, she said, "I want us to be friends. Can't we at least be friends?"

His groin stirred against her stomach, sending rockets of desire and surprise into her pelvis. She felt a flush on her chest beneath her dress, one that flooded upward into her cheeks.

He gave her a grim half-smile, then glanced away. "Friends don't feel what we're feeling, little miss school marm."

She swallowed hard and knew she should step away from him, but his words held her fast.

Hoping to slow her pounding heart, she took a deep breath. "What's happening, Sam? Why am I feeling this way?"

He studied her intently, his gaze moving over her face, her neck, her breasts. She felt a tingling everywhere, as if he'd actually touched her.

His grim half-smile returned. "You know why."

Amazed at her own audacity, she asked, "Please... tell me."

Watching her carefully beneath heavy, sloping, thickly lashed lids, he said, "It started that night by the fire, and you know it. I want you. I won't deny it. Every time I see you, I want to drag you against me and kiss you. I want to touch you in places I don't think you've ever been touched, I want to bury myself deep inside you, watch your face flush with pleasure, listen to your sweet sounds of contentment. In short, I want to take you to my bed and...and..."

Eve could hardly breathe. She found herself gasping, hanging on his every word, marveling at her ability to stay put and not run away. She hadn't imagined that men really talked to women this way. It was...it was as electrifying as if he'd physically seduced her.

Gracious and glory! Her body sang with desire and wonder, and she found herself asking, "And...and what, Sam?" Oh, she knew. She felt him, still stiff and hard against her. She was virginal, but she wasn't innocent. She'd read Hawthorne and Bronte and knew there was a sensual side to life that had, until now, eluded her.

Pulling her wrist from his grip, she rested both arms on his shoulders and gently touched the crisp, dark hair that hung below his ears.

She studied him carefully watching his eyes. The heat she'd initially seen was gone, replaced with something else. "You're purposely trying to frighten me, or shock me, aren't you?"

"It doesn't seem to be working, though, does it?" He released her, crossed to the fireplace and stared into the flames. "A woman like you shouldn't respond to that kind of talk."

Eve touched her chest, able to feel her heart beat beneath her fingers. "A woman like me? What...what does that mean?"

He turned slightly, giving her a thorough onceover, his gaze touching her everywhere. "A gentle-born school mistress who's never had a man between her sweet, milky white thighs."

Her pulse leaped into her throat, and she felt a jolt way down deep in her stomach. "You...you're trying to do it again. Shock me, I mean."

With a sultry half-grin, he asked, "You mean I still haven't succeeded?"

Wishing he didn't confuse her so, she went to the table and started cutting up the dried fruits and nuts for Christmas bread. "Why do you want to push me away?"

He turned back to the fire. "I've already told you why. If I don't, in the end, Joey will just get hurt."

She cut up a dried apple and dropped it into a bowl. "End? Just what 'end' are you talking about?"

Sam sighed and ran his fingers through his hair. "Do you have any idea what a woman usually does when she discovers I have a half-breed son?"

Eve thought she knew. She'd heard of a few women who'd been disappointed that Sam, the eligible widower, had an Indian child. "I'm not like that, Sam. I know what Joey is, and I think he's a wonderful boy. Bright, generous and maybe too sensitive. I think he's always going to have to fight for what he wants. Harder than other boys."

Sam was quiet. "So, you want to be my friend, is that it?"

She didn't like the sound of his voice. "Of course. And…and Joey's, too," she added as she dumped the fruit mixture into the bread dough.

"What happens when you marry your straightlaced white farmer? Or merchant? Or preacher? Then what? Will you still be my friend?" He turned and glared at her once again, his eyes sparkling dangerously.

She had to look away. The thought of marrying some anonymous stranger made her a bit sick to her stomach. In fact, she hadn't thought much about marriage at all. Well, that wasn't entirely true. Unwanted thoughts of Reverend Brewster murmured in her head, but that was useless thinking now. And really, it always was. Brief glimpses of a life with Sam and Joey flashed through her daydreams.

Her silence seemed to be his answer. "I didn't think so," he muttered.

"No, Sam. You don't understand. I... I have no suitors. No farmers, no merchants, no preachers." She shrugged a little and gave him a tremulous smile. "I've never had anyone really serious about me."

He studied her a long moment again, then answered. "It's probably because none of them think they'd have a chance with you,"

In spite of her nervousness, or maybe because of it, laughter burst from her throat. "And why not?"

His gaze grew heated. "Don't you have a mirror?"

"Of course," she answered, wiping her hands on a towel. She knew she was a comely woman, but at the orphanage she'd been told that looks meant little. It was what was inside a person that counted. "What's that got to do with anything?"

"You have the face of an angel and a body that would tempt a saint. Your hair is the color of the most perfect, pale wheat kissed by moonlight." He looked at her, the sultry smile slipping. Suddenly he wasn't smiling at all. "Tell me, is it that color everywhere?"

She swallowed, his intimation crystal clear. Trying to ignore the stirring between her thighs, she vigorously kneaded the bread. "You're trying to shock me, again. If you're not interested in me, why do you keep referring to my body parts? Do you think about them often?"

If Sam was surprised at her bold words, he didn't show

it. He simply gave her another heated half-smile. "More often than you can imagine."

Moistness gathered where the stirring had begun. "Then you didn't just say those things to shock me?" She tried to be calm as she braided the sweetened bread dough on a baking sheet,

He sighed and crossed to the window. "It doesn't matter why I said them, Eve."

She put a towel over her bread, then went to the stove and stirred the beans she was cooking for their supper. He was drawn to her, she knew it. He was also fighting it. Hard.

She pulled out the spoon and tasted the beans. They tasted all right, but she was so flustered, she couldn't be sure that she hadn't forgotten something. She turned to Sam.

"Um," she said, her expression doubtful. "Will you taste these? I think they need something else."

He came from the window, cupped his hand under hers and took a long sip of the broth. The touch of his warm, roughened palm on her hand sent tingles through her. She automatically took a step closer, and her breast brushed his arm. With quiet surprise she watched the desire that flooded his features.

Suddenly she knew she had some sort of power over him. The realization frightened her. She knew she could use it to her advantage, but she wasn't sure how. More importantly, she knew it was probably like a powder keg, just waiting to be struck with a match.

That evening when Sam stopped the sleigh in front of the Nisbeths', Eve shyly put her arms around him. She wanted things to be all right. She hated the tension that had arisen between them.

He stiffened, then pressed his fingers over hers, capturing her hand against his chest. "What in the hell are you doing?!"

Smiling at him in the darkness, she squeezed him hard. "I'm hugging you, Sam. I hate to see you so miserable, and if I'm to blame, I'm sorry."

He swore on a lusty breath of air, then pulled her close, kissing her hard.

Eve answered the kiss, anxious for it, needing it,

Suddenly he pushed her away. "You're to blame, all right. I can't seem to keep my hands off you."

Again, she felt the stirring inside her. "Is…is that so bad, Sam?" She could feel his gaze in the darkness.

"It could be the worst thing that ever happened to you."

His ominous words pressed against her heart. "I don't see how," she answered softly.

He jumped from the sleigh, went around and helped her out. "Trust me, Eve Engels... Trust me."

She left him and slogged through the snow, turning to watch him leave when she got to the house. Her insides were in turmoil. Something had happened tonight. There was an ache deep inside her. For somehow, she sensed that although what had occurred between them had felt right, it would ultimately cause them both pain. And still, despite the warning, it was the kind of feeling she couldn't ignore.

Once she was in her room, she heard a tap on the door. Oh, no, probably Cora. "Yes?"

The door opened and there stood not Cora, but her

niece, Trudy Harding. "We've hardly had a chance to get to know one another." Trudy had a mass of beautiful dark curls and a dimpled smile. Eve couldn't help but notice her generous curves.

"Oh, do come in," she said, actually eager for the company of someone closer to her age. "I've been so busy at the school with Christmas coming that I've hardly been here. Please," she added, "come sit." She was, after all, curious about the woman.

"Tell me about yourself. Cora says you've moved here from California."

Trudy sat gingerly on the bed, not completely comfortable. "Yes. I lived in a logging community. My husband died—"

"Oh," Eve interrupted. "I'm so sorry."

Trudy sighed. "Thank you. I stayed for a number of years, but then decided it was time to move on."

"And now you're here," Eve said. "How do you find things?"

"Fine. I've only been at the reverend's for a few days, but the children are adorable, and I love it."

Surprised, Eve said, "Really? You know, I deal with over a dozen children every day, but truthfully, being responsible for their total care is a bit overwhelming to me. Especially three little tots."

Trudy's face softened. "I never had children of my own, and I always thought I wanted a houseful."

"Well, if you wanted little ones, I hope things work out for you."

Trudy thanked her, rose and went to the door. "I'm glad

we could get to know each other a little, but I'm afraid I did all the talking."

Eve smiled. "Come to see me any time. And I guess you'll be baking Christmas goodies with us."

Trudy nodded, then turned to her. "The reverend believes it would be best for me to move into his sister's quarters, now that she's being treated for her illness elsewhere."

Curious, Eve asked, "What does she ail from?"

"Sadly, I believe she has been of frail health most of her life. Her lungs mainly. She is in Switzerland at a special clinic."

"Oh, but…I don't even like to mention this, but isn't that going to send everyone gossiping? I mean, surely you've heard what has happened to me."

"Yes, I've heard the wagging tongues," she said sympathetically.

Trudy sighed. "Believe me, before I came here, I gave the gossips a field day. I think I can manage this, if it happens."

Eve couldn't imagine it not happening, but then the reverend was a Godly man, well respected, so perhaps tongues wouldn't wag. "I really hope it works out for you," she added.

"Thank you, and I'm looking forward to doing some baking. Cooking is something I've learned to do very well."

"Well, then the reverend should be delighted to have you there."

Trudy's eyes sparkled. "Yes, I'm hoping so."

Chapter Seven

W hen Sam arrived home, he walked into the cabin and hung up his jacket. His gaze went to the table where the Christmas bread, or julekage, as she'd called it, lay beneath a neat, white cloth. Beside it were round ginger cookies sprinkled with sugar and a dried apple pie. The place smelled damned good. He glanced at the windows, strung with popped corn and berries, and over the mantel, where a sprig of cedar hung, a red ribbon tied to the top.

How he'd wanted to join her and Joey as they decorated the cabin. But it was foolish, this pretense of her being part of his family. Even if he might want it, it would never happen. He could dream about it from hell to breakfast, but it wouldn't happen. Soon, she was going to get tired of Joey. Tired of trudging over here to give him an education. Tired of cooking and baking and playing house. Yeah, it would be soon. Yet, remembering Joey and Eve together, making cookies, stringing popcorn, sitting side by side while she read to him, made Sam envious. Envious of his son's easy manner with her. And though he was very much afraid of it, he ached to have it last.

Grumbling, he went to the fireplace and slumped into a chair. His gaze caught her darning needle and thread, and he winced. In spite of his efforts to keep Eve at arm's length, he found her invading every corner of his space. It scared him. The empty gap inside his soul was growing smaller. He actually looked forward to picking her up at the school, though he couldn't let her know that. She had felt the same desire that he had when he'd kissed her.

He dug the heels of his palms into his eyes and swore. *Get control of yourself, you horny bastard*. Yeah, but it was damned easier said than done. If he didn't find a way to stop, he'd take her to his bed. And he had a strong feeling that she wouldn't fight him. Their coupling would be hot and sweet, intense and frantic. She looked like an angel, but he'd felt her fire.

He couldn't let it happen. Not ever. Because it wouldn't last, and when her proper Indian-hating friends found out about it, as they surely would, they'd reject her. And he couldn't purposely hurt her that way.

A part of him realized how easy it was to promise never to touch her when she wasn't around. Even so, there was an anxious urge deep inside him that couldn't wait to see her again.

He'd purposely tried to discourage her, certain that his crude innuendoes would send her scurrying away like a squirrel in the wake of bird shot. He smiled ruefully. She wasn't supposed to egg him on, no matter how innocently. Just the look in her deep blue eyes, that quiet expression of puzzlement and desire, had urged him to continue baiting her. She was the most delectable woman he'd met in a long, long time, and even though she was outspoken and sometimes bold, he was certain she was still untouched.

He rose from the chair and went to the bed, vowing he'd never again do something to make her think there was anything between them but gratitude and friendship.

But after he undressed and slid into bed, he could still hear the devilish little voice in his head laughing menacingly at his foolish promises.

The next afternoon, after her lesson with Joey, Eve wiped her hands on a towel and gazed with satisfaction at another fresh loaf of Christmas bread.

"Okay, Joey. Now you can sprinkle the *julekage* with cinnamon and sugar."

She watched as he carefully dusted the warm bread, using the precision of an artist to make sure every inch of the surface was covered.

When he'd finished, he stood back and studied his work. "How's that, ma'am?"

Eve watched the mixture darken slightly as it melted on top of the bread. "Perfect." She glanced at the clock set on the table by the window. "It's nearly time for Mr. Torkelson to pick you up. You'd better wash your hands."

Since Eve had arrived in the community, she'd heard nothing but negative things about Jeremiah and Mavis Torkelson. Clarence was always grumbling about "old man Törkelson's" refusal to sell his land so they could build a school. The commissioner of education had even come out from St. Paul with a generous offer, but it had been useless. Torkelson wouldn't budge.

Eve found it puzzling that the Torkelsons were so friendly and generous with Sam and Joey but shut out the rest of the community. Today, for instance, Joey was going over to their farm to help haul wood from the woodshed to the house. He would even be paid.

Sam still hadn't returned from his trip to town when she and Joey heard Mr. Torkelson's "hellooo." Joey quickly slipped into his jacket and pulled on his boots. As he stuffed his mittens into his pocket, he glanced at her.

"You want Mr. Torkelson to drive you home, ma'am?"

Eve gazed at the pile of dishes they'd used for baking. "No, that's all right, Joey. I'll stay and clean up. Your father can take me home later."

"Well," Joey said, gazing at the door, "I prob'ly won't see you for a couple of days, then. I'm stayin' the night. Mr. Torkelson says there's too much wood to haul for me to finish before dark." His face split into a wide grin. "Mrs. Torkelson is gonna make me a batch of fry bread. I ain't—I mean, I haven't—had fry bread and honey since before my ma died."

"Fry bread?"

"Yes, ma'am. We Dakotas love fry bread. Ever had any?"

Eve shook her head. "I can't say that I have."

"Maybe me and Pa can make you some. It's real easy, and it's good, too."

"I'd like that, Joey. Tell me," she added, "how did Mavis Torkelson learn to cook an Indian food?"

Joey shrugged. "I guess 'cause she's half Dakota, like me." He grinned again, then was gone,

Eve crossed to the window and watched Joey and Mr. Torkelson ride away. So, she thought. Mavis Torkelson was part Indian. Frowning, she wondered if that was the reason they kept to themselves.

She shook off thoughts of the Torkelsons, rolled up her sleeves and started cleaning up the dishes. She was just putting the last of the things away when Sam came in. She felt an immediate fluttering in the pit of her stomach.

He gave her a quick look, then hung up his jacket. "You still here?"

She'd hoped for a warmer welcome. Quickly looking away, she answered. "There were dishes to do. I couldn't just leave them."

He grunted a reply, went over to the basin and washed up. "You should have let Torkelson drive you home. Now I've got to hitch up my team again!"

She felt a rush of anger. "Oh, don't bother. It isn't quite dark, and it's only a mile. I can walk."

He cursed quietly. "You'd probably just get lost!"

Turning on him, knowing she'd wanted a different response altogether, she spat, "And that would suit you just fine, wouldn't it? Then I'd be out of your hair for good."

He crossed to the table and sat down heavily. "Yeah, then you'd be out of my hair, and I'd be relieved as hell never to see you again."

Eve turned away before he could see how his words affected her. She felt the foolish sting of tears and quickly overcame the need to cry. She didn't have to be struck in the face with a board to know it would hurt. And she didn't have to see Sam's face to know he'd somehow fought his desire for her and won. She might be stubborn, but she wasn't stupid. She fixed him a plate of supper, put it in front of him, then sat down across from him. "If it will make you happy," she started stiffly, "I'll continue to tutor Joey at school."

He gave her a questioning look.

Shrugging, she sighed and traced the faint pattern in the oilcloth with her finger, still feeling stupid tears pressing against the back of her eyes. "I'd hate to stop tutoring him just because…just because we can't seem to get along." She took a deep, shaky breath. It had all been so sweet, so wonderful. She'd had someone to cook for, bake for…care for. And love. All her life, it was what she'd wanted most.

But she knew now that nothing she did would make Sam love her. That had to come from him. If he didn't return her love, no amount of loving on her part could make up for the lack on his.

Suddenly she felt cold. Deep down cold, way into her bones. She shivered, stood and went to the fire. Even its warmth couldn't penetrate the depth of her chill. She'd grown to care for Joey so much, never mind how deeply she'd fallen in love with Sam. Had she really thought she could get to Sam through her cooking? She smiled sadly. Most men living alone would have fallen to their knees and kissed the hem of her skirt, had she cooked and done for them as she had for Sam.

A sharp gust of wind rattled the windows. She stepped closer to the fire and rubbed her arms.

"Wind's come up," he said from somewhere behind her.

She listened again and heard the continuous moaning

outside. "Not another blizzard, I hope." She didn't think she could stand to be cooped up with him again, especially knowing how much he wanted to get rid of her. She heard the scrape of the chair as he left the table and went to the window.

"It's clear. There's a cold moon up there."

"Well," she said, more for conversation than anything else, "that's a relief."

"Not really."

She pulled herself away from the fire and went to where he stood. She was tempted to lean into him, into his warmth. She forced herself to keep her distance. She peered outside, noting how moonlight bathed the landscape, accentuating the whiteness of the snow. "Why's that?"

"It's going to get cold. Real cold. It always does when the wind kicks up and there are no clouds."

She shivered again, sensing the change in the weather. "I…I think I should leave now."

He rubbed his neck. "No."

Fear lifted her heart. "What do you mean?"

"I won't take my horses out again."

She felt a brief bite of shrewish anger. "Your precious horses have more of your concern than any human."

"I need my horses. I don't need another human." He turned away and left her standing alone.

She spun around. "I don't believe you."

His slow smile surprised her. "I didn't imagine you would."

Irritated, she turned to the window again. "So, I'm forced to stay again, is that it?"

"I wouldn't suggest you try to leave. As long as you're

here, I'm responsible for you. I don't want Clarence Nisbeth lashing me to a post if you go out there and freeze to death."

She didn't want to stay. She wouldn't stay. She'd pretend to acquiesce, then, when he was asleep, she'd bundle up and leave. At least it wasn't snowing, and she'd be able to find her way home with the moon to guide her. "All right. I'll stay, but I'm really quite tired. Do you mind if I go to bed right now?"

He shrugged and nodded toward his bed. "Be my guest."

She watched him go to the door and let Chancy in, then bank the fire. After he'd climbed to the loft, she went to the bed, took off her shoes and slid under the covers, fully dressed. She dozed, then awakened with a start. Everything was quiet.

Slipping from the bed, she crossed to the ladder and listened. She could hear his heavy, even breathing. Relieved, she put on her boots, scarf and coat and crept silently toward the door.

Chancy whined and nudged her thigh, causing Eve's heart to leap into her throat. She knelt down in front of him, quietly ordering him to stay, then she slipped out the door, into the frigid, windy night.

Something awakened Sam. He opened his eyes, listening for the noise. Chancy. Rising up on his elbow, he heard the dog whine. He frowned. What was wrong with him?

He rose from the bed and pulled on his jeans, then

climbed quickly down the ladder. One look at his empty bed, and he knew what the dog was fussing about.

Cursing, he put on his jacket and boots, grabbed his rifle and a blanket and, with Chancy leading the way, strode outside.

He felt the harsh pinch of guilt as he trudged through the drifting snow. It was his fault she had left. He hadn't thought she'd be so damned foolish. He should have known that her pride would make her do it. She'd tried so desperately to cook her way into his heart, and when she thought she'd failed, she'd let her emotions take over. She had no way of knowing that she'd found a way to his heart the very first day he'd seen her, asleep in front of his fireplace.

He let Chancy go ahead, for the wind was so strong, there weren't even any footprints left for him to follow. The road was already indistinguishable from the ditches on either side. Great drifts were swept into frigid mounds, hiding the fences. If Eve had her senses about her, she'd be following the road, even though it was the long way around. Trying to wade through the snow in the fields would be impossible.

At Chancy's howl, Sam squinted into the distance, straining to listen. His heart drummed hard when he heard the distinctive snarling rumble of wolves. With a tight grip on his rifle, he forced himself forward against the wind.

Chapter Eight

S am approached carefully, quietly, his heart pounding. The wolves snapped and snarled as they circled Chancy. One of them lunged. With a fierce growl, Chancy threw himself at the wolf, seizing him by the neck with his strong jaws. They flailed and rolled in the snow, the other wolves in the pack snapping and yelping wildly.

The wolf suddenly slithered from Chancy's grip and plunged his teeth into his neck. Sam raised his rifle to fire at the wolf but didn't dare shoot for fear of hitting his dog.

Instead, he fired one shot into the air, then another, until the wolf who had taken Chancy down finally broke his hold, snarled menacingly and slunk away. The others followed, growling and yipping over their shoulders, their tails between their legs.

When he reached Chancy, the dog was still lying in the snow, panting. Sam removed his glove, reached down and pushed his fingers through the heavy fur at Chancy's neck. He drew his hand away; it was warm and sticky. Chancy was bleeding.

In response to Chancy's growling whimpers, Sam stroked his head, then moved his hand over the rest of the dog's body. He found no other injuries. "You're going to be all right, fella." When Chancy struggled to sit up, Sam dug into his pocket, pulled out a large bandana, and wrapped it around the dog's neck. "That'll have to do until we get home, boy."

Chancy pushed himself to his feet and stood, still whimpering, and padded deeper into the thicket.

Sam followed. They were far off the road now. He didn't want to think that Eve might have been tracked by the wolves and tried to take a shortcut through the field. But as he looked ahead of him, he knew that's what must have happened.

Chancy had stopped about twenty feet ahead of him and was bent over, nuzzling something deep in the snow.

Sam took the space between them in long heart-pounding strides. When he reached Chancy, the dog was bent over Eve, licking her face. Sam saw a log all but hidden in the drifts of snow. He was certain she'd tripped and fallen in her frantic attempt to escape the wolves. Now she wasn't moving.

Holding his breath, he knelt beside her and felt for a pulse at her neck. Relief rolled over him in waves when he found it strong and steady. He laid the blanket over the snow, gently lifted Eve onto it, then covered her.

She made a strangled sound and came awake abruptly, fighting him off with her fists.

"It's all right, Eve, Shh, it's all right," he murmured, drawing her close. She sagged against him and began to cry softly. Sam pinched his eyes closed and held her tightly, pushing down the emotion that clogged his throat.

Chancy yipped quietly beside him.

Pulling away, Sam slung his rifle over his shoulder, then took Eve into his arms. As he started back the way they'd come, he realized she'd gotten nearly a half a mile before she'd veered off course.

Once they were back in the cabin, he laid Eve on the bed, shrugged out of his jacket and then stoked up the fire. After quickly tending Chancy's wound, he returned to the bedside. Eve was coming around again, moaning slightly and moving on the bed.

He took off her wet coat, mittens and scarf and hung them by the fire. After sliding off her boots, he gently massaged her cold feet. She began to shiver. The hems of her skirt and petticoats were soaked clear up to her knees.

She stirred again and opened her eyes. "Sam?" Her voice came out in a quivering whisper.

Relief stirred inside him like a warm fire. Fearing she'd see more than he wanted her to, he pulled his gaze away. "Damn fool thing to do, Eve."

She continued to shiver. "Don't scold me, Sam. Get me warm."

"We'll have to get your wet clothes off. Roll to your side so I can unbutton your dress."

Instead, she sat up and eagerly helped him remove her wet garments. When they got to her underwear, she peeled off her camisole and with shaky fingers, unfastened her corset, tossing it onto the floor. Wearing just her chemise and drawers, she scrambled under the covers and huddled into a ball.

The load of guilt Sam felt for driving her away lay heavily upon him. She could have died out there. Either from the cold or by the wolves. Closing his eyes, he ran his hands over his face and shuddered.

He took a deep breath and gave her a questioning look.

"I think my drawers are dry enough to wear. I... I can't be sure though, because my hands are so cold."

Sam snaked his hand under the covers and touched her thigh. It was cold, but dry. How tempting she was, and how vulnerable.

"Well? Can I wear them?"

His hand moved slowly to her hip. Her rounded femininity stoked the fires in his groin. Ah, damn. He wanted to continue touching her, but he knew it would end in disaster if he did. Still, he allowed his palm to move slowly over her thigh to her knee, then back up again. He paused, waiting for her to stop him. She lay perfectly still. His hand traced the seam of her drawers from her navel to just above her soft mound, and he felt her sharp intake of breath. She began to shiver again but did nothing to stop him.

He was hard and ready but reveled in the twinges of pleasure and anticipation. God, how he wanted her. He swallowed, admitting to himself that he'd wanted her for weeks.

"S-Sam?"

He looked at her, his fingers resting on the soft mound of her womanhood. "Tell me to stop," he said on a hiss of breath. "Dammit, Eve, tell me to stop!"

She stared at him, still trembling, In the faint glow of light from the fire, he saw her grip her bottom lip with her teeth. Then she closed her eyes and slowly moved her legs apart.

Sam's heart drummed against his ribs as he slid his fingers toward her secret softness, to the open slit in her drawers. Down there, in the depths of her womanhood, she was wet and warm.

He stroked her, finding the hard bud of desire that pushed out through the swollen folds. She moved her head from side to side, eliciting sweet sounds that nearly drove him over the edge. He watched her face fill with the richness of passion as she moved toward completion. When he clamped his palm over her sweet mound, she dug her heels into the mattress, arched her back and cried out his name.

She lay there, her eyes closed as she caught her breath. Finally, she turned and gave him a tremulous smile. "I had no idea…"

Sam was ready to burst. He unbuttoned his jeans and slid them down over his long underwear. There couldn't be another explanation but insanity for what he was doing, but he wanted her. He wanted her.

He slid into bed beside her. She came to him willingly, anxiously. He touched her breasts, memorizing their shape again, then rubbed his thumb over one nipple.

She helped him remove her chemise, then brought his fingers to her breasts. He groaned when he touched them. "Soft," he murmured against her hair. "So soft." His desire for her grew, becoming a throbbing that tunneled deep into his gut.

She moved one leg, curling it around his, opening herself to him. They kissed, carefully controlled kisses that turned hot and slick. Eve knew what she wanted; she instinctively knew what he needed. He was hard and stiff. Reaching down between them, she clumsily unbuttoned his underwear, shuddering with pleasure when his length leaped out against her hand. She touched him, learning about him until he stopped her and groaned against her mouth. He pressed her onto her back. She opened for him and held her breath as he entered her,

"It'll hurt, but only briefly," he whispered against her ear.

"I don't care, I don't care," she answered, tossing her legs around him, pulling him in.

He drove deep, the brief bite of pain gone as quickly as it came. Then he grabbed her hips and held her tightly to him while he rocked rhythmically against her.

She felt it again, that surge of uncontrollable pleasure that made her ache with a joy beyond description. She shuddered, knowing that her own pleasure was made greater only by the sound of his. When it was over, he rolled to his side and took her with him. She reached up, pulled his mouth down to hers and gave him a long, sweet kiss.

"Sam," she said in a long whisper.

He drew her close. She sighed with contentment and snuggled against him. And for the first time in many years, she was happy to share a bed.

It was barely dawn when she woke. Sam stood in front of the fireplace, appearing to study the flames. Quivering sensations of pleasure touched her. "Sam?"

He turned briefly, then looked away. "I've got to get you home before it's light."

She flung the covers back, slipped into his shirt, and padded over to him, boldly putting her arms around him as she stood at his side. He tensed but didn't pull away.

"You're worried about my reputation."

He gathered her close and held her. "And your job."

Anxiety nibbled at her, but she refused to let it take hold. "What I do in my personal life is no concern of theirs." She wanted to believe it; she wasn't sure she did. Either way, she wasn't sorry for what had happened.

His hands framed her face, and he kissed her tenderly, a kiss that inevitably turned to fire. Her hands roamed his back, then his chest, where she hurriedly undid the buttons of his underwear.

His hands stilled hers.

"Please." She pressed her hands inside to his bare chest.

He sighed and pulled away. "Don't start again, Eve. I have to get you home before—"

"I know," she whispered, kissing his chest, "before it's light." She undid the buttons to his waist and pulled his underwear down his arms. He helped her get his hands loose, then allowed her to touch and kiss his chest.

"Oh, I knew it would be beautiful," she said, moving her face back and forth against the dark hair that covered him.

"Eve, Eve," he murmured huskily. "What am I going to do with you?"

She hugged him again. "You're going to do to me again what you did last night. But first," she added, pulling away, "I want you to find out for yourself."

His gaze was hot. "Find out what?"

She felt her heart pounding hard and knew she was being brazen. Slowly she slipped out of his shirt, letting it drop to the floor. "Whether or not my hair is the same color all over."

Sam stopped the sleigh far enough from the Nisbeths' farmhouse so that no one would hear it. He turned and looked at Eve. "Will you be all right?"

She glanced at the house; it was still dark. A chill scampered over her flesh, for if she were discovered sneaking in before dawn, she knew she'd be in real trouble. "I'll be fine," she squeezed his hand. "Don't worry."

He nodded, studied her briefly, then pulled her to him for a quick kiss.

Hunger for him returned. "Oh, Sam. I wish—"

He put a finger to her lips. "Don't, Eve."

She gave him a wobbly smile, then leaped from the sleigh and hurried toward the front door. She knew there were nights when everyone was asleep by eight or nine o'clock. And Cora no longer waited up for her to return from Sam's. She had discovered that one night when she'd returned just before ten and found everyone asleep, including Cora who usually waited for her in the kitchen.

Eve stole softly into the house. She stood for a moment, listening to the silence, when suddenly she heard Clarence on the stairs. He was always the first one up. Pressing herself against the wall, she held her breath and waited for him to go into the kitchen. When she was sure he'd gone, she quietly removed her coat and boots and slipped up the stairs.

Her room was cold. She removed her clothes, slipped into her flannel dressing gown and broke the thin layer of ice that covered the water in her washbasin. It really *had* gotten cold last night.

She'd just finished dabbing her face with the icy water when Cora knocked on her door.

With shaky fingers, Eve picked up the brush from her vanity table. "Come in, Cora."

Cora stepped into the room and looked around. "My, you're up early this morning."

Eve looked away and drew the brush through her hair with nervous fingers. "It was almost too cold to sleep."

Cora walked over and looked into the washbasin where little pieces of ice still floated on the water. "Don't tell me you didn't even go down to get the kettle of warm water off the stove."

Eve quickly put down her brush and took Cora's arm. "No, but now I'm freezing. Let's go down and have a cup of coffee, shall we?" Eve steered Cora toward the door just as she glanced at the perfectly made bed.

"Why don't I make breakfast this morning?" Eve offered. "I think it's my turn, isn't it? Clarence loves griddle cakes. Why don't I whip up a batch?" She squeezed Cora's shoulders. "Anyway," she babbled on, "it'll warm me up."

Before Cora discovered that she hadn't been in the room all night, Eve pulled her from the room and tugged her toward the stairs.

She felt a little guilty about the deception but also a flutter of excitement. She loved Sam, and although neither of them had voiced their feelings aloud, Eve was certain he loved her and would marry her. Then she could openly show the world the feelings that she'd kept hidden.

Chapter Nine

Later that day, Eve stood on a chair and struggled to attach a fresh cedar bough to the top of a window. The children had gone home, but the room was still filled with their excitement of anticipation for the Christmas program, which would be held soon.

Every now and then, when she was busy with something else, Eve felt a deep flutter of pleasure and briefly wondered why. Then she stopped what she was doing and remembered.

"Sam," she said on a soft smile. Her heartbeat sped at the sound of his name. He was a magnificent, loving, caring man, and he was hers. Or so she continued to tell herself.

Things between them were glorious now, but oh, how much more wonderful they'd be once they were married.

Stepping off the chair, she sat down, hugged her knees to her chest and smiled. She pictured Joey's reaction when Sam told him that Eve would be his stepmother. Oh, he'd be happy. But no one would be as happy as she would be. No one. Finally, she'd have a family of her own. A man to care for and love and a boy to watch grow into a strong, handsome man, just like his father.

Teaching was what she'd been trained for, but for as long as she could remember, she'd known that her ultimate goal was to have the family she'd lacked as a child.

She stood and dreamily glanced out the window. Her pulse raced when she saw Sam approaching in the sleigh, and she pressed her fingers to the base of her throat, feeling the throb of desire.

Quickly she donned her coat and boots and went outside. The brisk air felt good on her face, for through it, the sun was warm. Icicles hanging from the eaves had begun to melt, dripping in fat drops to the snow below. A fine layer of slick ice blanketed the snowdrifts.

She ran to the sleigh. "What are you doing here?" She couldn't keep from smiling; she was so happy to see him.

His face was solemn. "I came to make sure you were all right, and that…that no one discovered you'd been out all night."

Oh, how she loved his concern! Tears of love and gratitude filled her eyes. "No one found out. Oh, and I—" She caught her lower lip between her teeth, wanting to tell him she loved him, that soon it wouldn't matter if the whole world knew they'd spent the night together. But something in the rigid way he held himself stopped her. "I'm fine," she finally said around a vanishing smile.

He nodded, his eyes warm. "Want a ride home to the Nisbeths'?"

Laughing with relief, she climbed in beside him and slid beneath the blanket. "I'd rather go home with you," she answered shyly, resting her head on his shoulder.

"Joey's still at Torkelson's." It sounded like a statement of fact, not a seductively voiced invitation.

She felt a niggle of apprehension but ignored it. "I know," she answered, giving his arm a loving, knowing squeeze.

Sam didn't respond, but when they passed the turnoff to the Nisbeths' farm, Eve relaxed beside him and closed her eyes. This was where she belonged. It felt so right.

When they reached Sam's cabin, Chancy met them at the barn. Eve climbed from the sleigh, bent down and hugged the dog. "Hello, Chancy. You saved my life, you heroic dog." She glanced at Sam. "How is he healing?"

Sam opened the barn door. "He's going to be all right. Go inside, Eve. Get warm. I'll be in as soon as I take care of the horses."

Eve felt a giddy anticipation as she trudged to the cabin. Once inside, she removed her coat, boots and scarf and stood before the mirror over the commode, studying her reflection. Her eyes sparkled. Her cheeks were pink from anticipation as well as from the nippy air. She straightened the high, lace-trimmed collar of her cotton-batiste blouse, then ran her hands over her black cotton skirt. After pushing a wayward strand of hair back into place, she went to the hearth and stoked up the fire, Chancy at her side.

She put her hand on his head and gazed around the room, noting the ropes of popcorn and bittersweet berries she and Joey had made. They were draped perfectly over the windows and mantel. Joey's drawing of *The Christmas Cuckoo* was tacked to the wall beside the ladder going to the loft, and Eve decided that was the perfect place for other drawings Joey would make once he was in school.

She wrinkled her nose at the burlap window coverings. The flowered chintz fabric she'd seen at the mercantile would make perfect curtains. Surely Sam wouldn't mind if she put up something brighter and less dreary; after all, it would be her cabin, too. Oh, she wouldn't be extreme; she knew how men hated frilly, lacy things.

Her thoughts turned to Christmas Eve, just a few days away. She could almost picture Sam and Joey sitting on either side of her at the Nisbeths' supper table.

Just the other day she remembered Cora going on about their Christmas Eve meal.

"We always have a spartan Christmas Eve supper before church," she had told her. "Rice mush with cream and sugar, lefse and meatballs, if we have the meat. But Christmas Day…" Cora's face had become transformed when she thought about cooking and baking. "Ah, Christmas Day, we'll have lutefisk and turkey, and cranberry sauce and mince pie…"

Eve had not been familiar with those traditions because the nuns at the orphanage had drummed into her their more somber meaning of Christmas.

Sam came in and she ran to him, reached up and kissed him. She pulled away, gazing up at him. "I want to do that every day for the rest of our lives."

He gave her a tight smile but said nothing. He merely hung up his jacket and crossed to the fire, warming his hands. He didn't look at her.

Suddenly Eve was nervous. The niggling unease she'd earlier tried to ignore came back, stronger than before. With mounting trepidation, she went to him and put her hand on his arm. He neither responded nor moved away.

"Sam?" She was suddenly afraid.

"I should have dropped you off at the Nisbeths'," he said softly.

She swallowed hard, fighting the sick feeling that spread through her chest. "I didn't want to go home. I wanted to be with you." Quickly, before she could change her mind, she added, "I love you, Sam."

He swore and pulled away. "You can't love me."

Her nausea spread deeper. "But I do," she answered, barely above a whisper. This was wrong.

This wasn't the way it was supposed to be! He was supposed to ask her to marry him.

As though he'd read her mind, he said, "I can't marry you, Eve."

She pressed her hands to her mouth, crossed to a chair and sat down, his words of rejection ringing in her ears. "You can't, or… or you won't?"

He swung around and glared at her. "I'd ruin your life, and you know it."

She swallowed an hysterical laugh. Her life would be ruined if he *didn't* marry her, and not because he'd slept with her. She loved him. She wanted no other man. "Ruin… ruin my life? How can you say that?"

He turned back to the fire. "Do you want to be an outcast like I am? Is that the way you want to live?" Without waiting for her answer, he added, "I wouldn't do that to any white woman. How do you think you'd feel if everyone in this community shunned you? Turned away from you as you walked down the street? Whispered about you behind your back? Dammit, I know what it's like, Eve, and I hate it, but I'm used to it. You," he said, giving her a brief glance, "you wouldn't last a week before you'd despise me for destroying your reputation and your life."

She was dazed, stunned. "But... but after what we did, the way we felt..."

He sighed heavily and stared into the fire. "I'm sorry for that."

"S-sorry? You're sorry you made love to me?" Oh, God, this wasn't happening. It couldn't be happening.

"I am now, but I wasn't then. Hell, no." Suddenly he looked at her, his eyes intense. "At the time, dammit, I had to have you. With every breath I took, I wanted you. Thoughts of you wormed their way under my skin until I itched to bury myself inside you. I wanted to hear you scream out your pleasure. I wanted to stroke your sweet, soft skin. Kiss you everywhere... everywhere."

She stared at him, her heart beating madly as she remembered their night together.

He briefly closed his eyes and massaged his neck. "But I should never have done it, Eve. Because I knew that having you once would never be enough. Never having you again," he added solemnly, "will be my punishment for selfishly taking that precious thing that a woman can give only once. To one man. I shouldn't have been that man, Eve, and I'm sorry. I'm so sorry."

She stared at him; at this man she'd come to love so deeply. "You didn't take anything from me that I wasn't willing to give, Sam."

His tortured expression squeezed her heart. "What you want won't happen, Eve. I won't let it."

Stung, she answered, "And I have nothing to say about it?"

He shook his head. "No," he answered, so quietly she barely heard him.

Quickly, before she could think about it, she asked, "What if I'm…what if I—" She swallowed, feeling herself blush, but continued anyway. "What if I find out I'm going to have your baby?"

He turned, giving her a haunted look. "Then, by God, find yourself a good, hard-working man, Eve."

"*You're* a good, hard-working man," she cried out, on the verge of tears.

"I'm not good enough for you. If I were, I wouldn't have gotten you into this mess in the first place."

Trying to calm herself, she gasped for air. He'd never intended to marry her. Never. She pulled in a deep, shaky breath, unable to understand.

"But I *love* you, Sam. When you love someone, nothing else matters. It wouldn't *matter* if everyone avoided me. It wouldn't matter if they gossiped about me behind my back. I'd have you and Joey, and that's all I want. *That's all I want*, Sam."

He braced his arms against the mantel and stared gravely into the fire. "Go live your life as it was meant to be, sweetheart. I just hope I haven't already ruined it for you."

There was a heaviness in her chest. Her throat hurt. Her eyes stung. "Nothing I can say will change your mind?"

"Nothing," he answered, barely above a whisper. She stared at him, knowing that what she felt for him was stamped in her eyes, on her heart in her soul.

"I still want to tutor Joey. But . . . but maybe you should bring him and let me do it in the classroom, after the other children have left."

"If that's what you want."

Oh, my darling man, I want you. She crossed to the door and slipped into her coat. "I guess it's what's best." She couldn't bear coming here, to this place she'd hoped to call home, ever again. "Now, please, take me back to the Nisbeths'."

With a gruff sigh, he followed her. "The horses are still hitched up outside."

She valiantly kept her tears at bay. He'd known all along that he was going to reject her. She sat stoically beside him all the way home, but once she was in her own bedroom, she flung herself across the bed and sobbed.

The next morning was Saturday, and she accompanied Clarence and Cora to the mercantile.

While Clarence enjoyed a cup of warm rum with his cronies around the potbellied stove, and Cora supervised the filling of her shopping list, Eve wandered to the counter where the bolts of fabric were stacked. With sad eyes she looked at the brightly flowered chintz she'd hoped to use to brighten Sam's windows.

Two women began to speak softly on the other side of the wall that separated the fabric from the groceries. It was impossible for Eve to ignore them. "Well, if you ask me, she should be let go."

"She shouldn't have been hired in the first place," responded the other woman.

Eve frowned. She recognized their voices. They were mothers of two of her students.

"'I agree," the first woman said. "We just can't have that sort of thing going on here. This is a Christian community, not one of those savage reservations where God only knows what goes on behind teepee flaps."

Eve's stomach caved in around a bubble of nausea. She wanted to leave, but she stayed and held her breath.

The other woman sighed. "I just don't understand what got into Clarence Nisbeth. When he hired her…"

"Well, the poor thing was an orphan you know. I thought to myself, I thought, 'Gladys, we know nothing about how she was raised before they brought her here. That one's going to be trouble.'"

"You knew it right off, did you?"

"Oh, yes," the other said soundly. "Vain. That girl is vain with all that fair hair and, well, you know…she's got them curves that she don't even try to hide. Trouble. Pure trouble."

It hurt. Oh, how it hurt! Eve had never known they felt this way. Had she always been so naive, assuming that everyone liked her?

The other woman clucked her tongue. "Then I guess it's no surprise that she's taken a shine to that Prescott fellow."

"Can you imagine?" The woman's voice swelled with self-righteous glee. "Going after a man who has well, you know, *slept with a squaw*?" she finished in a loud whisper.

They both tittered nervously, and Eve could just see them, snorting like little pigs behind their lily-white hands. She hurt for herself, but it made her furious that they talked that way about Sam. Her anger came in the form of bold, hot tears that she had to force away with her handkerchief.

When she'd gotten control of herself, she squared her

shoulders, stepped out from behind the wall and stopped in front of them.

"Well, Merry Christmas, Miss Engels," one of them said with a shamefaced smile. "Are you and the children ready for the pageant? I know my Clarice is so excited to be the princess in *The Christmas Cuckoo* story."

Eve tried to force down her feelings of anger and hurt, but she wasn't successful. "Clarice will do a nice job. It upsets me, though, to hear the two of you talking so badly about Mr. Prescott. He's a fine man who is raising a child alone. Why must you condemn him?"

The two guilty women stumbled over each other's words as they hurried to get away from her.

Heat rushed into Eve's face as she went to the door, anxious to get outside where the air wasn't quite so foul. Her stomach was tied in knots. So, she thought, still fighting tears of anger, that was the sort of thing Sam and Joey had to put up with. People creeping about, pecking at them behind their backs in such a way that they couldn't defend themselves. Just how many people in the community felt as those two women did? Probably many. One was too many. They were eager for gossip but hid behind their pious outrage. It was awful, and it hurt. She didn't know how Sam could stand it. But she was sure it would be easier to withstand if he had someone beside him, giving him love and support. And she would have tried, if only Sam had asked her.

"Miss Engels?"

Startled, she turned to find the reverend watching her closely.

"Are you all right?"

She sniffed and got control of herself. "Reverend Brewster, good morning. I'm fine, thank you." She saw that he was alone.

He appeared to notice. "My sister is being treated for her weak lungs, and even when she returns, she won't have the strength to manage my little brood. I have permanently hired Mrs. Harding to care for the children. She handles them so well."

Eve relaxed and smiled. "I'm so glad. Trudy is such a fine woman." As she watched the man tip his hat and stride away, she recalled what Trudy had said about giving the townsfolk in the logging community a lot to talk about. But Trudy was so sweet. How bad could it be?

Chapter Ten

She was about to reenter the mercantile when she heard another voice. She turned to find a young man dressed in very nice clothing but his demeanor puzzled her. He appeared awkward and rather nervous. "Can I help you?"

"Ma'am, yes, ma'am. I'm hoping you can help me find someone." He fidgeted with his hat.

"If I can, of course," she answered. "Who is it?"

"Her name is Harding. Trudy Harding."

Behind his boyish looks were eyes like coal. Eve shivered. "What makes you believe she lives here?"

He ran one hand through his shock of blond hair. "A hunch, I guess. She said once she had kin here."

Cautious, she asked, "You knew this woman well?"

He snickered, not necessarily a pleasant sound. "You might say that."

Another shiver rippled through her. "I can't say I've heard the name, and I know most folks around here."

He sighed and looked around. "Well, as long as I'm here

I think I'll have a look see." He put on his expensive Stetson and turned toward the saloon.

Oh, dear, Eve thought, He'll certainly will find out better news there. She had to tell Trudy.

She turned toward the rectory, and in a rush, tripped over a loose board in the walking path. She went down face first. Hard.

Sam ran across the street in a flash. He had been watching the exchange from outside the livery. He hunkered down and gently rolled her onto her back. "Eve?" He lifted her into his arms just as Cora Nisbeth exited the mercantile. "Oh, my," she said in a rush. "Whatever happened?"

"She was hurrying down the sidewalk and tripped over a board," he responded, noting that Eve still had not opened her eyes.

Cora stood, wringing her hands. "We...we've got to get—"

"Pa! Pa! What happened to Miss Engel?" Joey cried, skidding to a stop in front of them.

"She took a bad tumble, son."

"The doctor must be notified, and we must get Eve home," Cora said, taking control.

"I'll get the doc," Joey said, wide eyed with worry. "I can run really fast." He raced off before he finished the sentence.

When Cora frowned, Sam said, "And he knows where you live, ma'am."

She blinked nervously. "Yes, of course he does."

At the Nisbeth's house, Cora sat in a chair beside the bed and watched Eve. The doctor said she may have a concussion, but he had checked her pupils, and they were equal. She stood and went to the basin to freshen a new cloth to put on Eve's forehead. An ugly bruise was forming above her eyes, creeping into her hairline. A shame to mar such a beautiful face. But Cora knew Eve very well. She would be distressed with the bruising but not because of her beauty but for the fact it might slow her down. And with her Christmas program so close, she would surely try to be up and about as usual.

Her thoughts wandered to Sam Prescott and his boy. Sam certainly seemed deeply concerned, even insisted on keeping her in his arms until they got to her room. And the boy, Joey. Tears had rolled down his cheeks and his eyes were wide as he watched the scene unfold. Yes, they both cared for her, that was obvious.

Eve stirred and squinted, her lashes fluttering. She groped around for Cora's hand. "What happened?"

"You tripped on a loose board in front of the mercantile," Cora answered.

Eve closed her eyes again. "I have a headache."

"The doc left some medicine for your pain. Should I get it?"

Eve nodded, but as Cora was about to leave, Eve said, "No. Wait. I must talk to Trudy right away."

Cora frowned. "Are you all right, dear?"

Agitated, Eve said, "Yes, yes. But please I must talk to Trudy now."

Confused, Cora thought for a moment. Trudy was moving into an apartment at the rectory. She had left early in the morning with some of her clothing in a suitcase. "She's at the rectory."

"Well, send someone over to get her, please," Eve pleaded.

Still not certain that Eve was really all right and not a bit muddled because of the fall, Cora told her she would try.

Eve watched Trudy's demeanor as she entered the room. Had she heard about the stranger? Oh, by the looks of it, she had.

Trudy hurried to the bedside. "Oh, Eve, what a tumble you took!"

"I'll survive. What about you?"

Puzzled, Trudy said, "Me?"

"So," Eve began slowly, "you haven't had a visitor?"

Trudy nodded, understanding. "Oh, you mean Travis? He's just someone from the logging camp I used to know."

"Why would he come all the way back here to see you?"

Trudy rolled her eyes. "Oh, he was stuck on me, but lordy, I was almost ten years older than he was. He was just a sweet little boy."

Eve remembered the dead eyes of that 'sweet little boy.' "What does he want?"

She rolled her eyes again, but a faint blush bloomed in her cheeks. "He thinks I ought to marry him."

Eve's jaw dropped. "Oh, really? Wh...what did you say?"

Trudy traced the zigzag pattern of the quilt on the bed. "I wanted to be kind, but what foolishness! I told him to go on home and find someone his own age."

"How did he take that answer?"

"Not lightly, I'm afraid. He said he'd be back tomorrow to see if I've changed my mind."

Eve touched her forehead and winced. "And tomorrow?"

Trudy let out a whoosh of air. "Heaven knows I will not marry the boy, but he knows certain things about me that..."

"That what?"

Trudy glanced at the window. "Things that, if misunderstood, could harm my reputation forever."

"Tell me," Eve said.

Noting the condition of Eve's face and realizing the pain she must be in, she said, "Oh, it's nothing. And you need to rest." She stood and patted Eve's arm. "Can I get you anything before I go?"

Eve suddenly realized that her headache was now pounding in her ears and out her eyes. "There's some medicine for pain on the chest by the wash basin. Could you bring it to me?"

Trudy did Eve's bidding, watched her take the medicine, then left. It wasn't long before Eve's eyelids were heavy, and she fell into a dreamless sleep.

It was a week until Christmas, and both Eve and the schoolboard decided the children could have a break from studies until the Christmas program was over. Eve had not argued. She felt all right, but she knew she looked like she'd been hit by a runaway six horse carriage. Her bruises were turning yellow and purple, and they extended over her face onto her neck. At least her eyes had not swollen shut.

When she left the house, she always felt pitying eyes on her, but she didn't care. She had tripped over a board, she had fallen and had fallen flat on her face and that was it. She hadn't lost an eye or severed a limb, for goodness' sake. She had heard a rumor that she must be devastated to have messed up her "pretty" face, but vanity had been whipped out of her at the orphanage.

As she sat by the window with her book, she saw that Sam's wagon had just pulled up and Joey hopped to the ground. Her heart beat rapidly at the sight of Sam, and she wanted to see him, but he sat on the wooden seat as Joey made his way to the door, holding a basket.

She pulled on a wrap, went to the door and opened it just as Joey stepped on the top porch step. "Well, hello, Joey, what a nice surprise."

He stood there, his mouth agape and his eyes wide. "Holy cow, ma'am."

She smothered a laugh. "Yes, I know. Did you come to visit?"

He looked back at his pa, then returned his gaze to her. "I…um…well, me and Pa, well, mostly me, thought maybe if we brought you some eggs you could…" He frowned and looked at his shoes. "But you ain't…aren't in any shape…"

Suddenly Sam was beside him. "I'm sorry. This was a bad idea."

She shivered. "Well, at least come in out of the cold." She opened the door to let them in, closing it behind them.

She felt Sam's gaze. When she met it, his eyes were filled with worry, not pity.

"I'm fine," she said, grateful for his concern. "The doctor said I don't have a concussion, and the startling display of colors across my face will eventually disappear."

"This was a bad idea," he said again.

Cora scurried into the room. "Visitors! How nice." She peeked into Joey's basket and saw the eggs. "Well, what a fine idea. We have dozens of Christmas cookies, but without eggs, how can we make any more?" She looked at Joey. "How about a trade?"

"Ma'am?"

"Well, I'll give you, say two dozen assorted cookies for the eggs you have in the basket."

Eyes wide again, he said, "Honest?"

"I think that's the going rate, young man." She held out her hand towards the basket, which Joey gladly gave her. "Oh, and there's a loaf of bread in there calling your name as well." Before she left, she said, "I think you should accompany me to the kitchen, young man, and pick out what you want."

Not having to be asked twice, Joey followed on her heels.

Eve nodded toward the sofa. "This may take a while," she said, hoping to hide her nervousness.

Sam sat, hat in hand and looked around the room. "Nice place."

She nodded in agreement, her heart still racing.

"Be hard to trade this for a rundown cabin, I would think," he said, as if to himself.

She narrowed her gaze. So that's how this was going to go. Somehow the smack on the face had hardened her a bit. "It would be like you to think so," she answered with nonchalance.

They sat in silence, but Eve looked at his proud, hard jaw, the thick coffee colored hair that was way too long and noticed that a button was missing from his shirt and she felt a tug inside her chest. Would anyone ever be asked to sew on another?

She took a deep breath and stood as Joey raced out of the kitchen with his booty.

"Look, Pa! Cookies and bread and even some home-made jam!"

Sam stood. "I hope you thanked her properly, Joey."

"Oh, yes," Cora intervened, "he has lovely manners."

Sam chuckled as they made their way to the door. "Yes, ma'am, when it comes to cookies."

"And Mr. Prescott," Cora added, "we can't thank you and Joey enough for getting the doctor so quickly and bringing Eve to the house."

He nodded, and they were gone.

She felt Cora's gaze on her. "What?"

"He is a nice man," Cora said.

Eve crossed to the window and watched them disappear down the road. "Yes. He is."

She pressed her hand over her stomach, praying it was her monthlies that were giving her anguish and not something else.

Sam felt Joey's energy beside him. "Can I have a cookie, Pa?"

Sam glanced at his son. "Can I stop you?"

Joey carefully opened the cloth covering and stared inside. "Want one?"

Sam put out his hand out, accepting the light, crisp cookie. After one bite he knew Eve had baked it.

Joey munched on his. "Miss Engels sure got her face busted up, didn't she, Pa? I wonder if she'll still be pretty when those bruises are gone."

Sam thought he knew Eve fairly well but did wonder if the bruising caused her any vainful anguish. "I imagine she'll look exactly the same," he answered. The same or not, there was an underlying beauty to Eve Engels that radiated from deep inside her into his very soul. Could he live without it? Did he really want to?

"Good. Good," Joey said, eyeing the basket of cookies.

"Go ahead, take another," Sam said as they rode toward home, "but I don't want the basket empty when we reach the cabin."

Chapter Eleven

Two days before the Christmas pageant Eve felt like her old self. Of course, she didn't look like it. She glanced in the mirror before leaving her room and grimaced. The shade of yellow blooming on her face wasn't becoming.

Suddenly there was a knock on her door. "Come in."

Trudy entered, her face white as she closed the door and pressed herself against it.

"What is it?" Eve was truly concerned.

Trudy released a shaky breath. "I don't know what to do."

Eve took her hand and led her to the bed. "I think it's time to tell me what's going on."

Trudy wrung her hands in her lap. "I hope you won't think too badly of me when I tell you."

Eve squeezed those restless hands in hers. "Just tell me."

Trudy pinned her gaze straight ahead.

"My Jerome and I had a good marriage," she began. "It's probably indelicate to admit that I enjoyed every part of that life, including the bedroom."

She stood and walked to the dressing table and casually lifted a jar of Eve's face lotion, not bothering to really look at it.

"He died so suddenly and so horribly—"

"Do you want to tell me how he died?" Eve asked.

Trudy shook her head and returned the jar to the table. "It was one of those mindless logging accidents, he was in the wrong place at the wrong time..." Her voice trailed off.

She seemed to gather some strength and paced the room slowly. "When he was gone, I didn't know what to do with myself. I always wanted children, but it just never happened. I had so much love in my heart; I just felt the need to share it." Her cheeks bloomed pink. "That's how it started anyway. The loggers are good men. Some are happy with their lives and some are not. After Jerome was gone, after all the men stopped by to offer condolences, a few of the men continued to come to visit. And because I didn't want to burden them with my pain, I would ask them about theirs.

"Some were dreadfully unhappy, and some just wanted someone to talk to, and I would listen."

"That doesn't sound so terrible," Eve said.

Trude expelled a huge sigh. "Sometimes one thing led to another, at first it was because I truly wanted to ease their pain, but...it always seemed to lead to the bedroom." She looked Eve directly in the eye.

Eve felt herself blush, for the innuendo was there. "Oh, I...I see." She didn't, not really, but she was in no position to judge anyone. A whisp of memory of her own indiscretion washed over her.

"The thing is, everyone knew it because men are just as gossipy as women. I became a pariah. The town whore."

Eve stood and went to her, placing her hands on Trudy's shoulders. "Oh, Trudy. I…I don't know what to say, except I'm sorry." She then gave Trudy a hug, and she nearly collapsed into Eve's arm and sobbed.

After Trudy stopped crying, she said, "And that's what Travis, one of the loggers, has on me. If I don't agree to marry him, he'll tell everyone, including Reverend Brewster, what I've done."

Eve's gaze narrowed. "I thought there was something sinister behind that boyish smile." She pursed her lips, thinking. "No matter what, you can't marry a blackmailer."

"I could do worse." Trudy's voice was barely audible.

"No! Don't talk like that."

"Well, what am I to do?" Trudy wailed.

Eve paused a moment then said, "You have to tell the reverend."

Trudy gasped. "What? No, I can't. He would think so poorly of me and kick me out for sure."

"Maybe not. After all, he seems like the sort of man who would look beyond it. Isn't there something in the Bible about this?" Eve had never been terribly religious, but she'd had her share of Bible lessons.

"Oh, you mean Mary Magdalene?" For the first time, Trudy actually laughed. "Well, I guess that's me all right, prostitute to the multitudes."

Eve gave her a generous smile. "Don't be so hard on yourself. After all, aren't men of the cloth supposed to forgive people?"

Trudy sighed and went to the door. "Thanks for letting

me bare my soul, Eve. What can it hurt to tell him? Either way I'll probably have to leave town."

Eve watched her go, crossing her fingers that the reverend was, indeed, a true man of the cloth. At least Trudy never got herself pregnant. Eve pressed her stomach again, wishing her monthlies would make their miserable appearance.

The night of the program clouds blanketed the moon.

Only a few stars peeped through the vaporous cover, offering little guidance to those who drove their sleighs toward the schoolhouse. In spite of the gloomy night, sleigh bells rang out, heralding the special evening.

The building was alight with candles and lanterns and could be seen from a great distance. The Hassler brothers and their wives and children had taken on the responsibility of delivering the lanterns early, so people could find their way.

In spite of her peculiar mood, Eve had to admit the schoolroom looked spectacular. The graceful red cedar tree, beautifully lit with candles, was a sight to behold. And the packages! Even though she'd told the parents not to bring gifts, she was sure they all had, for the floor at the base of the tree was loaded, as was a table nearby.

On every conceivable wall space hung pictures and sentiments suited to the occasion—big-bellied Santas, nativity scenes, trees laden with candles—while green cedar branches and colorful bittersweet berries graced the windows and door. From the ceiling, paper cutout snowflakes dangled on threads. Twenty or more stockings were hung on the wall beside the tree, each heavy with secret treasures.

The children were ready to perform The Christmas Cuckoo. Even Ernest Nisbeth, who played the king, knew his lines. Eve was uncertain, though, whether he'd say them correctly or turn the production into his own personal sideshow.

Eve briefly touched the delicate silver brocade brooch fastened to the lace at the neck of her blouse. Cora had loaned her the pin, for it went beautifully with the ecru linen blouse and skirt she wore.

She glanced around the room, filled with parents and their children, all of whom chattered noisily. She saw Trudy near the back with the reverend and his children, none of whom were yet school age. She waved at Eve and crossed the room to her.

"You're smiling," Eve noticed.

Trudy actually blushed. "You were right. The reverend is a forgiving man."

"And Travis?"

"He's gone. He has a nasty streak, but he decided not to tell everyone in town what had been between us."

Eve watched her return to the reverend and his brood. The reverend looked at her fondly. Forcing a happy smile, Eve stepped to the front of the room onto the temporary platform Clarence had erected for the program and looked out at her friends and neighbors. Briefly, since her confrontation at the mercantile earlier, she wondered how many were really friends. Someone near the front ordered everyone to be quiet so Eve could be heard.

When the noise died down, Eve clasped her hands in front of her and gazed up at the beautiful candlelit tree. "Isn't this the most beautiful sight?"

Murmurs of agreement rumbled through the room.

"I want to thank all of you for coming. The children have worked very hard, memorizing their lines for the production of *The Christmas Cuckoo*. Our beautiful cedar tree has an important part in the play tonight. It's not your typical Christmas story, but many of you know it well, since it's still told in the cold, icy north country of Norway."

There was a commotion behind the curtain, then Eve continued. "Briefly, this is the story of two brothers, the shoemakers Scrub and Spare, who inadvertently save the life of a cuckoo bird that they discover has magical powers. To thank them for his life, the bird offers them two trees. One is made of gold, and its leaves sound like coins when they drop off. Anyone who has that tree will be rich beyond his wildest dreams. The other is just a tree, but it is always green, and it never drops its leaves. Some call the latter tree a wise tree, others call it merry, for anyone who brings it into their home finds a happy, contented heart. Scrub wants the tree of gold. Spare, the merry tree. Let's find out which brother finds happiness."

Looking to the side, she nodded toward the boys who were ready to open the curtain. Slowly, the play unfolded….

"Eve, you've done a wonderful job," Cora said, giving her a hug after the performance. "I couldn't believe my Ernest. He said his lines perfectly!"

The disturbance caused by Clarence making his way through the crowd dressed as Santa Claus prevented Eve from responding. He stepped to the front, near the tree, and raised his arms to quiet the room.

"You children all did a fine job. A real fine job. Of course," he added, looking at Eve, "they couldn't have done it without a darn fine teacher who urged them on even after she took a wicked tumble in front of the mercantile. And I want to thank the Torkelsons, Jeremiah and Mavis, for donating those precious fruits they so cleverly stored in their cellar. Apples and all those delicious, dried fruits. He nodded to the couple who were seated toward the back.

In spite of her mood, Eve felt proud. Everything had gone perfectly. She should be elated. She knew why she wasn't…

Clarence tossed a casual glance toward the tree. "Now, I know the children are anxious for their treats and gifts. I've picked two fine young men to help me distribute them. But we have punch, coffee, Christmas bread and cookies in the back, too."

Eve scanned the room, her heart vaulting upward when she saw Sam standing toward the back, near the door. He looked so handsome. He'd shaved and his beautiful dark hair was combed back neatly against his head. Stubborn waves gave him a rakish look. With an ache in her heart, she wondered if she'd ever stop loving him.

He listened intently to a conversation between two other men, one of whom Eve knew was the commissioner of the school board, who had come in for the evening from St. Paul.

Sam's presence puzzled her. Not because he couldn't be

there. Everyone in the community had been invited. But…
why had he come? To finally get involved? To stop living
like a hermit? She hoped for Joey's sake it was true.

He looked up, as if sensing he was being watched, and
Eve nearly burst with a longing she wished would not come.
She held his gaze, perhaps drawing hope from it when there
was none. A flicker of a smile touched his mouth, and a
wealth of emotions made it hard for her to swallow.

Suddenly there was a disturbance near the door. A boy
rushed into the room, his face pale with fear.

"It's Ernie," he cried. "He's fallen through the ice on the
lake!"

Sam Prescott was the first man out the door.

Sam grabbed a coil of rope from his sleigh and ran
toward the lake. When he arrived, several boys were
standing on the frozen shore. He momentarily panicked
when he couldn't find Joey among them.

His gaze was drawn to the lake, his heart skipping a beat
when he saw Joey lying flat on the ice, next to the jagged
hole where the other boy had presumably fallen in.

"Joey? Are you all right?"

"Pa! I got Ernie by the hands, but I can't pull him out."

One of the boys on the shore ran up to Sam. "We'd
have helped, but the ice is cracked all the way around, and
we was 'fraid we'd all go through."

Sam nodded. By this time, some of the other men from
the schoolhouse were there holding lanterns, Clarence
Nisbeth in his Santa suit among them. Sam took control.

"We can make a chain out to Joey," he began, "but we'll
have to crawl on our bellies. Otherwise, the ice won't hold."
He made a hangman's knot in the rope and wrapped it

around his arm, then handed the rest of the rope to Clarence. "Follow me, then hand the rope back to the next man."

The human chain slid cautiously over the frozen lake. Sam heard the ice crack beneath them but prayed it was thick enough to hold. He focused on Joey, knowing he had to make it out there not only for him, but also for the boy in the water. As he crept closer, he hoped it wasn't too late.

"Joey," he called, "how's the boy doing?"

Joey looked up, his expression pained. "I'm talking to him, Pa, but he's crying. Can't you hear him?"

Sam could hear the muffled sounds coming from the hole in the ice. "Tell him his pa is right behind me."

"I did, Pa. He says he's real cold."

Sam reached Joey with a noose, then crawled to the edge of the hole. Looking down into the pinched face of Ernie Nisbeth, he gave him a reassuring smile. "We're going to get you out, son."

Suddenly there was a loud crack behind him, and Sam knew he was running out of time.

Eve tried to soothe Cora, who wanted to join the men at the lake.

"They have enough to worry about, Cora. They don't need to worry about us, too."

Cora squeezed Eve's hand. "Poor Ernest," she said, her chin quivering. "He's not really such a bad child, you know."

"He isn't," Eve murmured, vividly remembering the

time he put a nice, fat frog in her bed. And the dollop of molasses he'd poured on her chair. And the snake-shaped stick he'd wiggled at her last summer. Mischievous or not, no child deserved to freeze to death in icy water.

Some of the other mothers milled about, offering Cora words of comfort and encouragement. The children, sensing the tension in the room, threw curious glances at the tree and all the packages.

Eve was certain the festivities of the evening were over, when a few of the older boys rushed in, breathless from running.

"He's okay! Ernie's gonna be okay! They got him out of the lake, and his Pa is takin' him home!"

Cora sagged with relief against Eve.

Eve glanced at the doorway, her heart lurching upward when she saw Sam standing there.

"Mrs. Nisbeth, I'll drive you home," he said, taking her by the arm. He didn't even look at Eve before he left the schoolhouse.

Joey ran into the room and went straight to Eve. The sleeves of his jacket were wet to his shoulders.

When he peeled off his jacket, Eve could see that his shirtsleeves were wet, too. "I was hangin' on to Ernie's arms," he said, trying to warm his hands in his armpits.

Alarmed, Eve brought him to the stove. She rolled up his sleeves and rubbed his arms and hands gently. They were icy cold.

Eve was so proud of him, she wanted to hug him. Instead, so she wouldn't embarrass him, she gave him a warm smile. "That was a very brave thing to do, Joey."

He shrugged. "Somebody had to, and I was the only one who dared crawl out onto the ice."

Oscar Hassler went to the front of the room and called for everyone's attention. "Ernest is at home now, and the doc says he'll be fine. The Nisbeths want you all to continue your party. The youngsters have been eyeing those gifts something fierce, and it would be a shame if they didn't get a chance to open them."

Eve felt detached as she watched the evening progress. She sat near the stove with Joey, unwilling to think about her future. Her menses had not arrived, and she was never late. Never. There was a lump the size of an apple in her throat.

A while later, Sam returned with Clarence Nisbeth and went directly to Joey. They spoke quietly, Joey assuring his father he was all right. Eve couldn't help listening, wishing things could be different. Wishing she could respond to them the way her heart urged her to.

The boy who had announced Ernest's fall through the ice came up to Joey and handed him a package. Joey gave his father a questioning look before turning back.

"Want you to have this, Joey. If you hadn't crawled out and hung onto Ernie, he'd probably be dead now."

Another boy did the same, then another, until Joey had a lap full of gifts.

Eve felt tears press against her eyes and wondered why children were so often wiser than their parents. Joey looked up at his father, his eyes shining.

Sam gave Joey a smile that tore at Eve's heart. "Go ahead, son. Open them. You deserve them."

Eve could barely hold her feelings inside. She moved away, hoping distance would help dull the pain of losing

Sam. She crossed to where the other boys sat. "You've done a fine thing, boys. A very fine thing."

One of the boys blushed. "Joey done it, Miss Engels. Joey saved Ernie's life, even though Ernie was never nice to him."

"I know," she answered with a warm smile, "but—"

"I have something to say, and I want everyone to listen," Clarence Nisbeth called over the din. He threaded his way through the crowded room and stopped in front of Sam and Joey.

Eve held her breath. She prayed Ernest hadn't taken a turn for the worse.

Clarence reached out and touched Joey's shoulder. "We've all learned a lesson here tonight. Christmas is a time for giving, and this boy here, Joey Prescott, gave me back my son. If it weren't for him, Ernest would have drowned. And if it weren't for the quick thinking of his father, Sam Prescott, we might not have gotten to my boy in time." He studied them for a long minute.

The room was so quiet, Eve could hear the gentle sputter of the candles.

"We've all had our own run-ins with the Indians, and I'll be the first to admit I have a personal prejudice against them. But I'm willing to set that aside. What's done is done. This boy here," he continued, gripping Joey's shoulder, "is proof enough for me that it doesn't matter what a man's blood is. Good is good. Now, this boy's father has offered to sell us the land we need to build a new schoolhouse. At the time he made that offer, he knew darned well that we wouldn't take his son into this classroom. But I'm here to tell all of you," he added, "that we will. That is, if Mr. Prescott will forgive us all for being such narrow-minded fools."

Eve gasped, her gaze flying to Sam. She saw his shiny eyes. He was on the brink of tears. She pressed her fingers over her mouth and turned away before she made a fool of herself.

"Now," Clarence concluded, "let's go on with this party. There's plenty of eats left, and my Cora said no one is to go away hungry."

The boys who had given Joey gifts huddled around him, slapping him on the back, treating him like a hero. Eve dug out her handkerchief and wiped her eyes. Finally, Joey would be where he belonged in school with the other children.

Clarence stepped up to her. "Well, young lady, are you ready to go home? We all drew straws to see who cleans up, and the Hassler families lost."

She threw Sam a quick look, noting he was conversing quietly with Mr. Barnes, the carpenter. He didn't even look her way.

Dredging up a smile, she took Clarence's arm and headed for the door. "I'm ready." She squeezed him affectionately. "The apples were a big hit. And so were you, Santa."

He coughed nervously. "Well, of course." He studied her for a moment. "I'm not nearly the bear you think I am, Eve. Why, I might even be the kind of person you could confide in."

"Oh, I know that, Clarence. I know that."

"Well, then," he continued gruffly, "the next time you

come home in the wee hours of the morning, join me in the kitchen for a cup of coffee, and we'll talk."

She gasped, her face heating with a guilty flush. "You... you heard me?"

They stopped by the door, and Clarence helped her on with her coat. "Like I said, I'm not an ogre. I was wrong about Prescott from the beginning, and I had to do a lot of soul searching. But he's a fine man, Eve. You could do a whole lot worse."

Eve knew it too, but it was too late. If Sam had changed his mind about them, he'd have come to her and told her so this evening.

Chapter Twelve

E ve glanced up as Cora came into the room Ernest shared with his younger brother.

"Go to bed," Cora whispered. "I'll sit with him now."

Eve stood and stretched, yawning as she made her way to the door. She was tired but felt restless. As she passed Cora and Clarence's bedroom, the sounds of Clarence's rumbling snores made her smile. What a dear man he was.

She crept softly down the stairs to the kitchen to make herself some hot cocoa. Clarence had banked a fire in the stove, and the room was warm and cozy. The chime clock had just rung four. Later that morning, she and Cora would bake mince and dried apple pies and plum pudding and prepare the wild rice stuffing for the Christmas Day turkey. Tonight, after the Christmas Eve service, she would help Cora put the finishing touches on the children's gifts.

And tomorrow, Christmas Day… She sighed and lifted the pan of milk before it boiled over.

A noise behind her startled her. She turned and gasped. "Sam!"

He put a finger to his lips. "Come with me," he whispered. "Joey needs you."

She pressed a hand over her heart. "Joey? Oh, no. Is he coming down with something because of tonight?" Not waiting for Sam's answer, she hurried into the hallway and took her coat off the rack.

Sam ushered her outside into the waiting sleigh. He slid in beside her and spread the quilt over their knees.

"Does he have a fever? Chills?" she asked as they rode through the dark night. "Oh, Sam," she said, "maybe you should have called the doctor. I don't really know what to do. Oh, but I'm glad you came for me. I want to be there. Did he ask for me?"

"He never stops asking for you, Eve."

He sounded so calm. How could he be so calm? A wrenching, emotional pain twisted her stomach. "The poor darling. Oh, Sam, why did you leave him alone? Are you sure he'll be all right?"

They were approaching Sam's cabin; a tiny light flickered in the window. He'd barely drawn the sleigh to a stop when Eve leaped down and ran into the house, Sam following close behind her.

She threw off her coat, slipped out of her boots and hurried to the loft ladder when she felt Sam's hand on her arm. Puzzled, she turned and faced him. He had the strangest smile on his face,

"What... what's wrong? Sam, I have to go up there and see how he is—"

"He's fine. All you'll do is wake him up, Eve."

"But...but I thought you said he was calling for me."

Sam folded her into his arms. She went willingly, but she was confused.

"He's always calling for you. Not a waking minute goes by that he doesn't ask me why you aren't here."

She pulled away. "He's not sick?"

He gave her a shy, apologetic smile. "No."

She continued to brace her hands against his chest. She felt the beat of his heart, which surely matched the drumming of her own. "Then…then why am I here?"

"Because it's where you belong."

She sucked in a shaky, optimistic breath. "Your little prank scared me half to death. I'm very angry with you, Sam Prescott."

He bent and kissed her forehead. "Too angry to become Mrs. Sam Prescott?"

More emotion than she could hold filled her, and tears ran down her cheeks. She gave him a tremulous smile. "No, I'm not that angry."

"I was wrong, Eve, to deny our love for each other. After tonight, and the way the townspeople rallied around us, publicly supporting Joey and me, I realized how wrong I'd been." He pulled her to the center of the room and pointed to the ceiling. "It's not mistletoe or holly, but it will have to do."

Eve glanced up at the bittersweet berries that hung from the ceiling on a string. She gave Sam a loving smile. "All that for me?"

His grin was lopsided. "Joey thought it was a good idea."

He bent and kissed her, the sweet kiss turning hungry.

Pulling away, he framed her face with his hands and looked into her eyes. "If I keep kissing you, I'm going to want to take you to bed. But I won't. Not until we're married."

She pressed close, craving the desire that surged through her. "Oh, you're such an honorable man."

He hugged her tightly. "You don't sound too thrilled."

She rubbed her cheek against his shirt. "The biggest part of me isn't. But I still maintain a kernel of decency, in spite of myself."

They stood quietly for a long minute, then Sam said, "I suppose I'd better ask Clarence Nisbeth for your hand, or he'll string me up by my heels or by something else more precious to both of us."

Blushing, she laughed shyly, remembering her revealing conversation with Clarence. "I wouldn't worry, Sam. When he discovers that I'm gone, his first thought will be to give me away, and with good riddance."

Joey awakened shortly after five a.m. and didn't appear at all surprised to find Eve there. While he and his father went out to the barn to do chores, Eve prepared breakfast.

They'd barely finished eating when they heard the jingle of sleigh bells. Eve and Sam exchanged glances.

"Joey, go help Mr. Nisbeth with his team."

Joey flashed his father a puzzled look. "How do you know it's him, Pa?"

Sam stood and began clearing the table. "Trust me, Joey, it's him."

Joey pulled on his coat and went to the window. "I'll be dogged. You're right, Pa."

As soon as the boy went outside, Eve hurried to the window. Clarence Nisbeth stopped his team in front of the cabin and handed Joey the reins. He looked at the house, his expression stern. She checked to make sure there was enough coffee, then quickly rattled the cookie tin, grateful it wasn't empty. Clarence never took a cup of coffee without eating something sweet with it, even if it was just after breakfast.

She felt Sam's hand in hers and gripped it hard.

Clarence entered, greeting them both solemnly. He took a seat at the table, motioning Sam to sit across from him. Eve poured him a cup of coffee and put it down in front of him, next to the plate of cookies, then sat next to Sam. When Clarence cleared his throat, she felt her insides quiver.

He took a molasses cookie, bit into it and gave her a look of approval. There was a twinkle in his eye that told her he was prolonging her agony on purpose.

"Stole her away in the middle of the night, did you?"

Sam nodded. "Yes, sir, I did."

"She came willingly?"

"In a manner of speaking."

"He told me Joey was ill," Eve said, shooting Sam a scolding look.

"I didn't say that, you did."

His eyes were so warm and deep, she almost drowned in them.

Clarence poured some coffee into the saucer, blew on it then slurped it into his mouth. "You going to marry him?"

Eve glanced at Sam, unable to stop smiling. "I am."

Clarence slapped his knee then stood. "Thought so. Saw Reverend Webster on my way over. Said you'd already talked to him. That right, Prescott?"

"Sam?" Eve couldn't believe it. "You talked to the reverend? When?"

He pulled her close. "Last night after the pageant."

She melted against him. "You were pretty sure of yourself, weren't you?"

Clarence cleared his throat gruffly. "I hope you two can wait a spell. Cora wants all of us to attend Christmas services tonight, and she fully intends to see that you, Sam, and your boy, join us for Christmas dinner. Guess she wants to kinda look you over. See if she approves."

Eve flew to him and kissed his cheek. "They'll be there. Oh, Clarence! You are a wonderful man."

Clarence gave her a fatherly hug, then opened the door to let in Joey, who had hitched the reins to the post.

Clarence paused and smiled at all of them. "So, she's your angel, is she? Then I suppose you know what 'Engels' translates to from the Norwegian?"

Joey stamped the snow from his boots. "What? What's her name mean, sir?"

Clarence cuffed Joey lightly on the chin. "Why, it means 'angel,' son."

He beamed at Sam. "See, Pa? I knew it. I knew the first time I saw her that she was an angel."

"And now she's going to be your new mother, Joey."

His face lit up, and his grin was so wide, Eve thought his mouth would crack. "No kiddin'?"

"No kiddin'," Clarence mimicked. He turned briefly to

Sam and Eve. "Cora would feel slighted if you two didn't tie the knot in our parlor. You're like a daughter to us, Eve."

Eve's heart felt full to overflowing. "Oh, Clarence, thank you. If anyone's an angel, you are."

He studied her quietly. "I don't want to tell you what to do, girl, but Cora's got a heap of cooking to do today, and I think she's expecting your help."

Eve's hand flew to her chest. "Oh, yes. Oh, of course, Clarence." She tossed Sam a worried look.

"Go on. Joey and I will be along later," he said, helping her into her coat.

She turned and hugged him. "You promise?"

"We promise. Nothing could keep us away."

"Ma'am?"

Eve turned to study Joey. "Yes, Joey?"

He started to stutter and looked around the room then cleared his throat. "Um, I don't know what I'm supposed to call you now."

Eve bit back a wide smile. "Well, you can't keep calling me ma'am, can you?"

He blushed. "No, ma'am."

"What would you like to call me?"

"Well, since you're marrying my pa, would it be all right if I called you Ma?"

Eve bent down in front of him and took his face in her hands. "It would make me happier than you can imagine."

His face split into a wide grin. "Me, too."

They hugged.

"In two days, you will be my ma," Joey announced.

⁓

Two days later, Sam and Eve stood at the window and watched the Nisbeths leave. They had insisted on transporting them to and from the wedding ceremony and keeping Joey at their place for a few days. Although Joey did protest, Ernie Nisbeth, who was now so grateful to Joey and Sam for saving his life, promised him they would finish the huge snow fort that was becoming a mini house in the backyard.

"Well, how do you feel, Mrs. Prescott?"

Eve snaked her arm around Sam's waist and rubbed her cheek against his chest. "I feel like the happiest and luckiest woman alive." They were quiet for a moment, basking in the newness of their relationship.

"I never did get you anything for Christmas."

Eve stretched and kissed his chin. "Oh, yes you did."

He brought her full against him and held her. She felt his need; it matched her own. Earlier, as they accepted good wishes from their neighbors in Clarence and Cora's parlor, Sam had read the urgent hunger in her eyes. "I know, sweet angel," he'd whispered against her ear. "It's the same for me." She'd wanted him so badly, she thought she would burst into flames.

"I mean," he said, interrupting her thoughts, "you don't even have a wedding ring."

"Oh, Sam. It doesn't matter. All my life, Christmas had meant very little to me. In the orphanage, we didn't really celebrate it. We were expected to go to church, but other than that, we did nothing special. I remember visiting a friend from school over Christmas once, and her family had a Christmas tree, piled so high with presents you could barely see the top. How happy they all were to be together!

The traditions they'd shared over the years… I suddenly realized what I'd missed. Yet her family wasn't mine, so it just made me sad. Then Clarence and Cora took me into their home, and I've shared their traditions and been grateful for them, but they still weren't mine.

"Now," she said, hugging her husband close, "I have a family of my own, and the traditions we start will be ours. Not only that, but my wedding day is the day after Christmas. How much more special can Christmas be than that?"

Sam pulled away and tipped her chin toward him. There was a soft gleam in his eyes. "And every Christmas, will you bake those ginger-and-molasses cookies?"

"Of course, darling." She gave him a suggestive smile. "Didn't you know? Ginger is the spice of love."

Sam returned the smile, then glanced toward the loft. "I'm glad Joey's staying with the Nisbeths."

She snuggled close, removed the stiff collar of his shirt, then unbuttoned it. She pressed her hand inside against his chest, near his heart. "If he's gone for too long, I might miss him."

He unbuttoned her dress, pausing now and then to kiss the sweet flesh that he revealed. "I'll keep you too busy for that."

She shuddered as he drew his tongue over the top of her breast. "Oh, Sam. Joey's had so much excitement in the last two days… I'm so happy for him for you… for me. For us."

Sam slipped out of his shirt, then drew her dress down over her arms. "I know. I don't know how Joey and I got so lucky."

"Silly man," she scolded softly, trying to unfasten his trousers. "I'm the lucky one. Now," she said, pulling him toward the bed, "I think we should be sure I have the start of a baby in my belly."

"A start? You mean…"

She nodded. He gave a soft, delicious laugh and followed her. "I hear you, sweetheart. Let's make another little angel."

About the Author

Jane's first historical romance, *Secrets of a Midnight Moon*, was heralded as 'sensitive and sensuous, violent and tender.' "I found the plot to my first novel in a little-known history of Northern California Indians when I learned that Native Americans were being taken as slaves by the settlers, their families threatened with death and dismemberment if they tried to leave. Yes, one can weave a romance around such an appalling event!" Since then, she has published thirteen full-length novels and four anthologies, all dealing with the perils and passions of romantic historical fiction.

She graduated from the University of Minnesota majoring in American and Russian History revealing that, "while all of my stories are set in the US, I had hoped one day to set one in Russia, though in my opinion, the best ones have already been written."

Jane continues to write and also edits for Melange Books, LLC. She currently lives in St. Paul, Minnesota with her husband, Richard Noer.

THANK YOU FOR READING

Did you enjoy this book?

We invite you to leave a review at your favorite book site, such as Goodreads, Amazon, Barnes & Noble, etc.

DID YOU KNOW THAT LEAVING A REVIEW...

- Helps other readers find books they may enjoy.
- Gives you a chance to let your voice be heard.
- Gives authors recognition for their hard work.
- Doesn't have to be long. A sentence or two about why you liked the book will do.

Also by Jane Bonander

The Runaway Wife

The Bedroom is Mine

Joey's Angel